C. H Fretwell

The Story of an Ancient Mariner

Being Reminiscences of Seafaring Life Half a Century Ago

C. H Fretwell

The Story of an Ancient Mariner
Being Reminiscences of Seafaring Life Half a Century Ago

ISBN/EAN: 9783337415204

Printed in Europe, USA, Canada, Australia, Japan

Cover: Foto ©Andreas Hilbeck / pixelio.de

More available books at **www.hansebooks.com**

THE STORY

OF AN

ANCIENT MARINER.

BEING

REMINISCENCES OF SEAFARING LIFE

HALF A CENTURY AGO.

BY

CAPTAIN FRETWELL

(AN OCTOGENARIAN).

London :

S. W. Partridge & Co., 9, Paternoster Row, E.C.

1892.

PREFACE.

I DO not know how many times I have been requested to publish a narrative of twenty-five years of my life as a seaman, an officer, and commander of ships in the Merchant Service of our country, and beloved Island Home—that country which has produced some of the boldest mariners and navigators the world has ever seen.

It may seem strange to some readers that an octogenarian should, after the lapse of more than half a century, undertake to relate his long past experiences. I am well aware that the readers of the present day are more inclined for stories of fiction than biographies, though the latter are better calculated to improve and leave a healthy impression on the mind; nevertheless, I venture to launch this little book, hoping it may prove an encouragement to some young aspirant to an adventurous life on the ocean, or a cautionary voice to others who are about to set sail on the voyage of life. If so, the writer will feel well rewarded.

C. H. F.

CHAPTER I.

IT is my intention to pass over, as briefly as possible, the first four years of my seafaring life, only mentioning some of the most striking incidents and accidents so rife in the experience of those who "go down to the sea in ships."

My first voyage dated from September, 1824, when we sailed from the port of Hull to St. John's, New Brunswick. We started in stormy weather which obliged us to put into Lerwick, one of the Shetland Islands, where we remained three days; afterwards the weather was very fine, and we arrived all safe after a passage of thirty days.

The numerous trials and severe hardships which sailors had to endure at sea some seventy years ago will scarcely be believed now-a-days; I proceed, however, to relate some of those which early befell me.

The ships were bad, the lodgings were bad,

B

and the master and mates were hard task-masters. In those days they were not called captains and officers, for few of them were educated men, being only a degree better than common "Jack." The provisions, as a rule, were of the worst and coarsest quality, the salt beef was hard to digest, and, perhaps, the hardest of all was the biscuit. Dogs of the present day, brought up in the lap of luxury, would shy at it. There were no missions to seamen, there was no Miss Agnes Weston to provide suitable homes for Jack ashore; no benevolent Plimsoll to survey the ships before leaving port. Happily for the present genera-tion of adventurous youths, all is changed for the better. But having made my choice, I was resolved to abide by it without murmur-ing or discontent.

I have nothing of special interest to relate on this first voyage with the exception of two narrow escapes of my life. On one occasion I was ordered where I ought not to have been sent, because of my inexperience in climbing so high on the rigging—the main top gallant yard. My head began to swim, my strength failed, and a fall of sixty feet into the sea seemed imminent. Nevertheless, the yard was lowered down, and after resting

AN EARLY EXPERIENCE.

for a few moments on that giddy height, which I can never forget, I recovered strength and came down from aloft, safe and sound. The other adventure was less dangerous on account of my being a good swimmer. I fell into the water from the quarter boat, a distance of about sixteen feet. The ship was lying at anchor in the harbour, with a strong tide running; the weather being so cold that the thermometer registered seven degrees below zero.

The homeward voyage was accomplished in safety, and our heavily laden ship, after a stormy passage, arrived at Hull about Christmas time, and thus terminated the voyage.

In the year 1825 we made two voyages to the same place. Crossing the Atlantic in the early spring there is considerable danger on approaching the great Bank of Newfoundland, extending as it does over four hundred miles out to sea. Here the great cod fishery is carried on, which supplies with salt fish the Mediterranean and other ports. In addition to stormy weather, frequent fogs occur, and icebergs of enormous size, which are sometimes very numerous, are met with. The greatest vigilance is essential on the part of the commander, officers, and crew, all eyes being brought into requisition for the general safety. I have crossed the seas between England and North America twenty-six times, and must pause here to give my grateful testimony to the goodness and mercy of God, Who, during all these voyages, preserved me so signally from "perils in the sea." How many ships have gone down with all on board, not one being left to tell the story! Until the sea gives up the dead, will their sad secret remain undisclosed!

We left St. John's in January, 1826. The cold was so intense that frequently the thermometer registered thirteen degrees below zero. Coming down the Bay of Fundy, we were caught in a severe snowstorm, and in handling the frozen sails I got frost-bitten in both hands and feet. The ship was taking in over her bows heavy seas of fresh water, which froze and became a solid body of ice forward, rendering the performance of our duties most arduous, until we reached the open sea. It is marvellous how the salt sea moderates both heat and cold. A fierce wind and cyclone continued, with but little intermission, all the way across the Atlantic, a period of twenty-one days.

Having arrived home, the ship was laid up

in the dock during the winter, the boys being kept at work to refit her for the spring voyage.

The next voyage commenced with brighter hopes and prospects; we were bound southward into more genial climes, but alas! the hardships of the young beginner did not slacken. At the end of March we sailed for Norfolk, in Virginia, which was the great centre of the slavery then prevailing in the Southern States. The entrance into Chesapeake Bay is formed by two headlands, Cape Henry and Cape Charles; Baltimore stands at the head of the Bay. The beautiful rivers, Elizabeth, Potomac, and Susquehannah —leading on to Washington, the capital— discharge their bright waters into the Bay. Everything here teemed with animal and vegetable life; snakes were very abundant, and the brilliant fireflies at eventide had a pretty effect; but the croaking of frogs all night, in concert with the negro melodists, "made night hideous."

My hard fate—almost as bad as slavery— was to work with the negroes in loading the ship with heavy masts and bowsprits of pitch pine, and with hiccory and locust treenails for the British Navy.

Before completing our lading, the fiftieth anniversary of the Independence of the United States came round, and two such remarkable coincidences never happened in the history of the great Republic as occurred on the 4th day of July, 1826. The deaths of two of the ex-presidents, John Quincy Adams and General Jefferson, took place on this day. Mr. Adams, who, with General Washington, signed the Declaration of Independence, had been for several days in a state of coma. Awakened by the noise of bells ringing, and music, he asked the cause, and was told it was Independence day. He then enquired about the health of his friend Jefferson, and was informed that he was dying, to which he rejoined, "And I too shall die to-day." Yankees never do things by halves, they go the whole hog, vulgarly speaking. A mock funeral service was performed in every large town in the Union —a grave was dug in each cemetery, a hearse containing a coffin was followed by a long procession of carriages, in which mourners were seated, thus completing an imposing *cortège*. I am sorry to add that much drunkenness and dissipation took place among the lower orders in the evening, but on that I need not dwell.

Virginia, as before observed, was then the great centre of the slave trade, and we had many negroes on board helping to load the ship. Though only a boy at that time, I had many conversations with them on the subject of slavery, and its iniquitous practice of treating human beings like animals. I well remember three stout, strong fellows—workmen in my gang. They were the property of a widow-lady, who was kind, although she appropriated all their earnings, one dollar each daily, giving them food, clothing, and lodgings (if such they could be called, in the compound). I asked if they were happier here than in Africa, at Anamaboa (I knew the place); they all replied in the affirmative, and with strong expressions. I inquired, "Suppose the good lady were to die, what then?" A pause ensued, and the tears shone in their eyes, and then the answer came, "We should be sold and separated for ever; now, sir, we be like brothers." This fact convinced me, young as I was, that slavery was an abomination in the sight of God, Whose hands have made and fashioned both black men and white, and Who "is no respecter of persons."

Having completed our lading of the ship, we set sail again for Plymouth. The passage home proved long and tedious, lasting nearly two months. On entering the English Channel, we were 300 miles out of our reckoning—so much for the navigation of that period! After discharging the cargo at Devonport dock we were ordered home to Hull, our voyage to America and back occupying almost an entire year. What a change in our day!

It must not be supposed, when the ship was laid up in dock, that the apprentices were allowed to rest. They had all the rigging to overhaul, and tar down from the mast head to "the dead eyes," and to paint and scrape off the pitch from the sides and bottom after the caulkers. On arriving home for breakfast one morning, after being thus engaged, my face and hands spotted, looking not unlike a negro who had had small-pox, I sat down to a hearty meal, and was in the act of leaving when a servant called out, " Please, sir, be good enough to leave that cushion behind you!" The cushion had adhered to my tarry clothes !

In the year 1827, about April, we set sail for Archangel, in the White Sea, the " land of the midnight sun." After leaving the latitude of the Shetland Islands, we used no artificial light all this voyage. At midnight the sun was about ten degrees above the horizon, and the heat at mid-day was very great. The mosquitoes were ravenous, worse than in India; one boy was sent to the hospital in consequence of being bitten all over. The beef here was only twopence per pound, and of the finest quality I ever tasted.

About three hundred ships came into port in one week to load grain, and timber for building purposes. The Russian officers in the Custom House were terribly dishonest, nothing being done without a bribe. Collector, comptroller, and subordinates were all tarred with the same brush. You ask to see one, in order that you may enter the ship inwards, but to no purpose; he remains invisible until you show the sclavonic—a ten rouble bill.

We were only three months making this voyage, and then sailed again for Miramichi, in the Gulf of St. Lawrence. There I first became acquainted with Mr. Cunard, who established the famous line of sailing packets between New York and Liverpool. In after years we met again, and our acquaintance ripened into friendship. It is well to recall some bright experiences amid the dreary routine of crossing and recrossing the ocean, often lashed into angry billows which seem ready to swallow up the frail barque in their relentless embrace. " Fire and hail, snow and vapours, stormy wind fulfilling His Word."

I must not omit to mention here a remarkable instance of the power of prayer in connection with this line of sailing packets. Mrs. Cunard was a very godly woman. It is related of her that when any of the ships sailed from New York or Liverpool, she was accustomed to retire to her room the whole day, and spend it in prayer. · The sceptic may scoff, if he please, nevertheless the fact remains that this line never lost a ship, nor even a man, during her life-time, a period extending over ten years !

The remainder of this voyage, followed by two others from Hull to Miramichi and back, closes this part of my story.

CHAPTER II.

IN those days of competition advancement was most difficult, either with regard to the command of a ship, or to the obtaining of any situation on board. Then, as now, a man had to labour for his living.

Knowing this, I started for London to seek my fortune, having only a few pounds in my pocket, and there I encountered fresh trials, and greater difficulties in the struggle to obtain employment of any kind. Ships in commission were scarce, and sailors plentiful. How well do I remember walking up and down this modern Babylon, with its crowded streets; men and women hurrying along in eager pursuit of something, whilst I, though surrounded by this great multitude, felt as much alone as if lost in the depths of a vast forest, or wandering on a barren heath, "weary and worn and sad." I visited all the docks and shipping in the great metropolis, but there seemed no

chance for me, every berth was occupied. After a
month or two of fruitless efforts, I chanced one
day to dine at the "Bull and Mouth" Hotel,
in Aldersgate Street. It was about half-past
two in the afternoon, the large tables were
empty with the exception of one gentleman at
the further end of the room, who sat with his
face buried in the newspaper, until I had finished
my repast. On discovering who it was, I
exclaimed with delighted surprise, in the words
of Hamlet, "Oh, my prophetic soul! My
uncle!" He was a merchant, and had a good
connection in London. Within a few days he
introduced me to Alderman Humphreys, who
afterwards became Lord Mayor. It so happened
that an old friend of Mr. Humphreys' had just
taken the command of an Indiaman, bound to
the Cape and Bombay. He gave me a letter
to the captain, which I delivered myself, upon
which he promised me a birth in the ship,
The Boyne. But it was only before the mast—
all the four officers being engaged. I well
remember telling my uncle that if only I could
obtain employment, my services would soon
procure me advancement.

I have always regarded this circumstance as
a special interposition of God on my behalf,
thus opening up a wide field for labour,

.THE "BOYNE" LEAVING ENGLAND.

enterprise, and promotion. Some may deem
it trivial, but " Trifles make the sum of human
things " ; and, as John Wesley was wont to
say, the world was his parish, so now I could
realize for the first time that the world was
before me.

When the time came for signing articles to
engage the crew, more than two hundred
seamen were there, and only fifty were required. But for the letter of introduction to
Captain Warren, I should have lost my chance.

The voyage to the Cape and Bombay
commenced in September, 1829. With a cargo
of merchandise, and the full complement of
first-class passengers, we proceeded down the
river to Gravesend. Here, though very un-
willingly, I must mention an experience which
I would fain omit altogether, but I am bound
to give my readers a true picture of the state
of things at that time. The ship was two or
three days going down to Gravesend, there
being no steamships then. The sailors had
received their month's advance of wages, and
were followed by a motley group of land
sharks, crimps, and women of the lowest
character from Ratcliffe Highway, Old Gravel
Lane, and Wapping. All the way the ship
was more like pandemonium than anything I

c

ever witnessed before or since. Finally, the
pilot ordered all the women out of the vessel.
This order fell like a bomb shell; but though
the night was dark, there was no resisting it.
They did not clear out, however, without
uttering the vilest imprecations upon his head.
Of course such a disgraceful state of things is
not now permitted.

We called at Plymouth to take in the
captain and passengers; decorum, strict discipline, and order, taking the place of wild
disorder.

About the fourth day we sighted Madeira.
By and bye we came near the equator, and
the sailors busily employed their spare time
in preparing to perform the shaving trick on all
who had not previously crossed the equinoctial
line. This custom, now happily obsolete, was
allowed in those days, and a most barbarous
one it was. I forbear describing what took
place—having had to suffer the penalty myself
—and gladly bury it in oblivion.

On further proceeding towards the Cape of
Good Hope, we encountered a very suspicious
looking schooner sailing round about us for
two or three days, which the captain, officers,
and passengers, all took to be a pirate. The
movements of this rakish-looking craft were so

PREPARING FOR THE PIRATE.

strange and unusual, that we all set to work to prepare for an attack, either by night or day. We had already heard something of a cruising pirate being dangerous hereabouts, and prepared ourselves for a fight, having two cannonades, muskets, cutlasses, and boarding pikes. She came very close, however, one day, and getting alarmed, as we supposed at our strong force, gave up the attempt, and we lost sight of her in the night to our great satisfaction. This was really fortunate, for we found afterwards none of our shot would go into the cannonades, and as for our other great guns, they were only shams, painted to look warlike. Jack used to call them Quakers, because Quakers do not fight, but their formidable appearance just answered our purpose, and probably saved our lives.

This story of the pirate is no myth, for I saw the same schooner lying without her masts in St. Helena Roads; she had been captured meanwhile by a cruiser in the British Navy, and condemned. The captain and some of the vile crew escaped, but three of them were hanged on the Island of St. Helena. They were supposed to be Portuguese from their language and appearance.

There was a good band of musicians on

board, which tended to relieve the tedium and monotony of a long voyage.

The men in the forecastle were arranged in messes of eight each, one being appointed cook for the day. I had to take my turn with the others and draw the provisions and grog, wash up dishes and platters, and sweep all clean below.

As a little time, say half-an-hour, was allowed after performing these duties, I generally slipped away into some quiet corner to read my Greek Testament. The captain alone knew who I was, but he took no special notice of me until I had made my mark as a steady, trustworthy sailor. However, before very long, he ordered me to come on the poop deck and take charge of the boys and midshipmen, This was a rise to be petty officer, though I still had to remain in the forecastle. The middies were separated from the crew. The sailors called them "bread-room mice," because they had no wages. Jack used to say the midshipman's half-pay was three farthings a year, and he drew it quarterly!

Although my rise did not place me among the officers of the ship, yet very shortly after it gave me an opportunity, if I may so speak, of distinguishing myself. It happened on this wise. One fine day when the ship was sailing very fast, with a fair wind and all sails set, suddenly a cry was heard, " a man overboard!" At this alarming sound the watch below and the passengers hastened on deck to witness the terrible sight of a man struggling for life. The helmsman rushed to cut away the life-buoy, but had no knife. Time was precious. At last the buoy was dropped into the sea some distance from the man, who could not swim. Quickly a boat was lowered from the ship's side. I was the first man who volunteered, with only two others, to encounter the stormy waves. After rowing a mile or more, guided by the life-buoy, I stood on the stern-sheets of the boat and espied on the top of a wave the man's head and fiery red hair (which was of the greatest service in effecting the rescue) at some distance from the life-buoy. Just as he was sinking for the last time I caught hold of him at arms' length below the surface of the water, and we pulled him into the boat exhausted and apparently lifeless. I laid him on his stomach across the boats' thwarts, when he vomited a large quantity of salt water. On being taken on board, the doctor applied the usual remedies. He soon became conscious, and ere long was restored to his usual health. This boat was in my charge, and the incident appeared to me a favourable augury for the future, gaining as I did the applause of the captain, officers and passengers.

CHAPTER III.

DURING the remainder of the passage to the Cape we were favoured with most beautiful weather, running the South-East Trade winds down, as it is generally termed, and at length arrived at Cape Town, Cape of. Good Hope. I remember being on shore on Christmas Day —it was midsummer there. I was much engaged in boating and conveying . the passengers on shore ; about half of them were landed, one being Colonel Wade, who afterwards was made Governor.

Having made an exchange of passengers, and filled up all the vacancies, we proceeded towards Bombay. I leave it to the reader's imagination to suppose what a change this was to me, so recently come from the cold regions of the North Atlantic. We caught a number of sharks, porpoises, dolphins, flying fish, and albicore; also inferior fish, scarcely eatable, except that sailors living entirely on

salt provisions are glad of any change. I
remember we captured one very large shark.
We were particularly interested in ripping him
up, and carefully examining the contents of
his stomach, · expecting to find a watch or
jewellery undigested. A lady, looking on, said,
" What are you going to do with this
monster, Jack?" To which the sailor replied,
" Why, eat him of course! If I were in his
way would he not eat me?" This was quite
in accordance with a sailor's argument, the
lex talionis. If Jack has been taken in by
crimps at Liverpool, he travels to London
and takes *them* in there, repaying them in
their own coin.

Sailing. along the coast of Malabar, we got
into the sea and land breezes alternately day
and night. I have known the sea-breeze about
noon so strong that it was blowing. half a
gale, while the sun was shining brilliantly in
a cloudless sky. The difference between the
Atlantic and Pacific Oceans is expressed. in
the name of the latter, which signifies "peace-
ful," or free from storms.

My mess-mates, as well as myself, had now,
comparatively speaking, an easy time of it, and
some of the sailors related some remarkable
yarns. One was by an old man, a mess-mate

in this ship *Boyne*. He had been sixty years on the water, having gone to sea when only ten years of age, but, being no scholar, he never rose beyond a foremast man. In the year 1788 he went out to Botany Bay in the first squadron of war and transport ships, taking out the first convicts to that settle-. ment. There he saw a white man among the savages, who had run away from the *Endeavour* (Captain Cook's ship) in 1765. He was offered a free passage home to England, but declined. He had become so changed by his nomadic life as scarcely to be distinguishable from the savages, and had almost forgotten his own language.

The *Boyne* was now lying in the harbour of Bombay, the passengers having all been taken ashore. We commenced discharging her cargo—about one thousand tons of merchandise of every description suitable to the Indian trade. Bombay is an island on the Malabar coast, standing in a bay, which forms one of the largest and finest in our Indian possessions, capable of secure anchorage for a thousand ships.

The cholera was raging there at the time to a fearful extent, and from two to three hundred of the natives were dying off every week. Some of our seamen on board had it, causing the captain to be very much alarmed, but he used every precaution for the preservation of the health of the crew, and we did not lose a man. The heat was intense, at times something like a hundred degrees in the shade.

I visited the island of Elephanta and saw the wonderful subterranean caves filled with barbarous images for worship of the most ghastly description, carved out of the solid rock. I also saw a fakir at Mar-ma-dell Tank, who had held a flower-pot in his hand for over seven years; his finger nails had grown six inches long, having the appearance of twisted horny substances. This was a penance imposed upon him by the Buddhist priests for some crime he had committed.

The ship having taken in her cargo of Indian goods, we set sail with a full complement of passengers for London, calling only at St. Helena for water and a fresh supply of stores and provisions, the deprivation of which we had felt ever since a severe hurricane had swept the deck, carrying away all the live stock.

I satisfied myself as to the truth of the particulars about the pirate before alluded to, and found all to be correct, the same craft was still lying there as a warning to all who entered upon such diabolical practices on the high seas.

We arrived at length at the East Indian Docks in London. This voyage must have been a profitable one for the owners, as the ship was always full of passengers, and had a full cargo of goods both out and home ; notwithstanding this, the men were kept out of their wages for fourteen days, at the expiration of which Jack had either spent or lost all his money, living on credit as he must have done, after toiling hard, and encountering the dangers of a long sea voyage.

CHAPTER IV.

ITH all my economy and self-denial I soon found myself with very slender means, and only a doubtful prospect of improving my circumstances. So long a time elapsed before Captain Warren obtained his next appointment that I resolved to return to the North American voyages, and had actually shipped on board the barque *Mary Anne*, of St. John's, New Brunswick, drawn a month's advance, and purchased my sea-stock of warm clothing, intending to join the following day, when on arriving at my lodgings at Poplar, near the West India Docks, I was most agreeably surprised to find my brother Tom, a seafarer like myself, sitting in the back parlour.

"What in the world are you doing here?" I exclaimed.

In the course of conversation it appeared he had been in London more than a week trying to find me out, until one day, after dining at a restaurant, the room being cleared, he told the proprietor of the fruitless search he had had after his brother, without any clue or address. The man's attention was arrested, and looking at him, he said, " I think I can find him for you. He comes here frequently to dine, and judging by the similarity of your appearance and voice, he must be the very person you want, for you are as much alike as two grey peas." He directed my brother to my rooms, but I was out when he came. Later on in the day, however, we met. That same evening I received a letter from Captain Warren, offering me a berth as fourth officer in the *Exmouth*, bound for New South Wales.

Notwithstanding my previous engagement, I decided to accept Captain Warren's offer, when it suddenly flashed into my mind to give up my situation as second mate of the *Mary Anne* to my brother Tom. Most willingly did he agree to this proposition, and as there was no time to be lost he went on board the following morning and began to work, without saying a word to anyone. The impersonation was so complete that the exchange was never discovered. I am not now justifying my line of action in this emergency, but it suffices to say, for the present, that he was a seaman, a scholar, a good navigator, and that he became a commander before he was twenty-three years of age. However, I am not telling his story but my own, and must therefore revert to the *Exmouth*.

These events proved to be the turning-point of both our chequered lives. "The Lord reigneth"—the Highest of all beings is best of all. Our lives are one unbroken testimony to His watchful kindness. May we hear His voice speaking to us in every providence. From this period my brother and I seemed to emerge from hard labour and servitude into comparative ease and comfort, and, although the result of our thus meeting together was a separation for many years, we could not feel otherwise than thankful for the turn which events had taken.

Being engaged as the fourth officer of an Indiaman, I was placed on an equal footing with the other officers, and passengers. The very next day I was commissioned to enter on duty, and to be aide-de-camp to the chief officer.

Mr. Grayson, my chief, was a first-class seaman and officer; he conducted all the affairs relative to the management of the sailing, besides taking the supervision of the officers and crew. The captain's attention was chiefly directed to the passengers and to securing their comfort. A strong intimacy soon sprang up between Mr. Grayson and myself. We were the only two officers engaged for about two months in preparing the *Exmouth* for a voyage to the Antipodes. My pay was very good, which enabled me to appear well dressed and in uniform, and I was qualified by previous experience to give orders to the men with fullest confidence. I may say Jack has a special aptitude for finding out where an officer has received his training in early youth.

Outward freights direct to India were rather scarce at that time. Our ship was ordered to Woolwich to fit out at Her Majesty's dockyard, preparatory to taking out convicts to Sydney, New South Wales. Being thus equipped as a prison-ship, we embarked two hundred and ninety convicts, including sixty boys, for this penal settlement. The crew consisted of fifty sailors, with officers and servants, and a guard of fifty soldiers, including a captain and four lieutenants, also a doctor appointed by Government.

The *Exmouth* was a ship well appointed in

D

every respect for the conveyance of such a living freight of rascals, gamblers, and dangerous characters not fit to be at large in any civilised community. The change from the hulks to the colony, or penal settlement, was in favour with all. Those who behaved well on the passage were recommended to settlers as assigned servants to work out the term of their imprisonment, receiving threepence a week with food and clothing. This small sum was given to prevent them from being regarded as slaves on the estate.

The discipline on board was rigid in the extreme, and punishment by flogging resorted to for trifling offences, insubordination or disobedience. I saw one case of this kind where three convicts were flogged over the bare back with three dozen stripes apiece. It was an awful sight, but it kept them in subjection all the voyage. We left Torbay on the 17th March, 1830, and arrived at Sydney in ninety days, this being considered an average passage, for it is a distance of about fifteen thousand miles.

On our journey we overtook another convict ship near the Equator, with women on board. This vessel proved to be in a leaky state. I went on board and saw the women passengers working at the pumps. It was "pump or

SPERM-WHALE FISHING.

sink" with them. Proceeding further, we
boarded a South Sea whaling vessel, alongside
of which, hanging on the tackles, was a monster
fish. The crew were flinching off the fat and
boiling it on board. It was a sperm whale,
the oil of which is very valuable. The brain
was pumped out of the head and looked like
spermaceti salve. From the same animal is
obtained, what is called, ambergris—a very
fine scent. This is secreted in some part of
the body, as musk is in the civet cat. There
was also a live whale in the sea, almost as
large as the ship itself, playing about the
vessel with the greatest ease imaginable.
Some of these sperm whales have yielded one
hundred barrels of oil, worth one thousand
pounds. This animal belongs to the mammalia,
has warm blood, brings forth its young and
suckles them, but it has now become almost
extinct. The supply of this oil having failed,
other kinds have been developed, such as
petroleum, or rock oil, from which paraffin is
extracted; here we see the goodness of
Providence in providing us with an excellent
substitute when the old stock fails.

Finally we passed through the Straits,
arriving at Sydney—one of the largest and
safest harbours in the world; sufficiently

spacious to hold the fleets and merchant ships of all nations. Without delay, we disembarked our living freight and housed them in barracks.

If the histories of the lives of some of these unhappy men were narrated, they would fill volumes. Some had been well educated and had moved in the upper circles of society, but drink and impurity had made them lose all self-respect, and caused them to become companions of men sunken in sin and degradation.

The ship was lying at anchor off a rocky islet in the stream called Pinchgut, not a euphonious name, but one which was given to it on account of a desperate character who had been confined there in heavy irons, and who had died of starvation. Here I had frequent opportunities of visiting the creeks and coves, botanizing, and decorating the ship with azaleas, pelargoniums, geraniums, and ericas—one of the latter, called the native rose, is of surpassing beauty—growing wild. This island of New Holland, as it was formerly named by the Dutch, and by Captain Cook, New South Wales, is that which is now known by the name of Australia. The Irishman calls it the fifth quarter of the globe. The climate is extremely salubrious, and the scenery all around magnificent. The island is in circumference six thousand miles, and I travelled round it from Torres Straits, Western Australia, called Perth, including Swan River towards the great gulf of Carpentaria. Its flora and fauna, and its sylvan groves present many new features to the observer. For instance, the birds, although clothed in brilliant plumage, have no song, the flowers no fragrance, the bees no sting. The dogs are dumb, the cherries grow with the stones outside, and the swans and cockatoos are black. The pears are solid wood with the thick end near the tree. The Australian crow is a splendid bird, capable of being taught to imitate any sound like the mocking bird; his feathers resemble the magpie's, and are black and white. There is also the platypus, or water-mole, with the bill of a duck and spurs like a cock. Some of the convicts of whom I have been speaking, who left their country for their country's good, have turned out to be industrious men, and even ornaments to society.

CHAPTER V.

THE vessel having been thoroughly cleaned and painted, we left Sydney for Calcutta, in convoy of several ships and a frigate, to go through Torres Straits, which separate New Holland from New Guinea. This attempt was a failure, for the north-west monsoon set in, and we were driven back and compelled to go round by Tasmania. Having lost an anchor and cable, it was not considered safe to prosecute our voyage to India without replacing them, so we put into Hobart Town, the capital, situated on a very charming estuary called the Derwentwater. This was also a convict settlement, though, to my mind, far too lovely and grand a spot to be inhabited by such persons. Some of the red gum trees here are of gigantic size, supposed to be six thousand years old. All the trees are evergreen, not deciduous, and some shed their bark yearly. Here again I was permitted to roam about enjoying the lovely scenery.

How delightful it is to look upon Nature, where we see God's work clothed in all its beauty, cultivated and nurtured with the utmost care by the hand of man. One specimen, in particular, that I cannot fore-bear mentioning is the Dollicas, a creeper or clematis, which covered three sides and the roof of an outbuilding with its thousands of mauve petals, surpassing every sight in the floral kingdom I have ever beheld; shall I say with one exception? for I once saw at Cadiz the heliotrope cover the whole front of a house, from the base to the eaves in full blossom, with this addition that the perfume pervaded the atmosphere for some distance.

Tasmania has no rival in climate, salubrity, bright skies, and the fertility of its soil, unless it be New Zealand. Snow falls sometimes here, but seldom lingers more than a few hours.

Having heard a curious story about an animal found in these regions, the *dacyurus ursinus*, apparently belonging to the genus named sloth, but by colonists called "devil," on account of its very ugly appearance and obnoxious habits, I determined to try to see it. So I walked about two miles to a nursery plantation, where one was confined in an iron cage. I knocked- at the door of the curator's house but without gaining admission. At length the proprietress came; I told her my errand, upon which, without any appearance of surprise, she addressed a manservant in these words, "John, show this gentleman the devil." I saw him, and in all my travels I never remember to have beheld such a revolting object.

We had to beat round Cape Lewen, the most westerly point of New Holland, against stormy winds and heavy seas. We were conveying horses to India, which are most troublesome in stormy weather as they never lie down; therefore we were obliged to sling them up by the middle in order to keep the weight off their feet. Finally we entered the Bay of Bengal, and passing the Nicobar and Andaman Islands, sailed up the river Hooghly, a branch of the Ganges, and entering Garden Reach—a little paradise of tropical beauty, with a botanical garden on one side, and on the other fine mansions of rich nabobs—we came to an anchor off Calcutta, "the city of palaces."

The *Exmouth*, being a ship well known in

India, soon obtained a full freight of goods
and passengers, including many distinguished
Europeans returning home on furlough, or
retiring from the service.

On the passage home we had the misfortune
to lose Mr. Grayson, the chief officer, who,
without any sign of previous illness, was found
on the floor of his cabin, having died suddenly.
He was the most important man on board,
and all the passengers were grieved at his
unexpected death. Speaking for myself, I lost
one of my best friends. This event placed
me in charge of his watch, and gave me the
position of third officer. Fortunately I had
had much experience as a seaman, and having
profited by his training, I was duly entrusted
with this responsible post. We called at St.
Helena for water and provisions, as usual on
these voyages, and arrived safely in London,
after landing the passengers at Southampton.

St. Helena once belonged to the East India
Company, but when their charter was abolished it reverted to the Crown. I happened
to be there when the ceremony took place,
which was on the occasion of the appointment
of the new Governor. He was saluted by a
great firing of guns from the forts on the
island, which were responded to by all the

ships in the harbour; for about twenty minutes the whole welkin resounded, the cannon echoing and re-echoing through the hills and valleys with deafening noise, like a war of the elements. In my journeyings up and down the South Pacific from Africa, India, and China on the homeward voyage, I have called there for water and refreshment eight times.

I once rode up to Diana Peak, two thousand feet high. This is Longwood, where Napoleon lived when in exile, and I saw the open grave whence his remains had been disinterred, the bricks and stones forming the vault were loosely scattered about; even the house he had occupied was turned into a cattle shed.

I remember one day while taking the sun's altitude to find the latitude, I observed an eclipse of the sun. After a strict search in all our nautical almanacs, we found it was not recorded. This incident gave me somewhat of a reputation as an astronomer. Leaving this historical place we sailed up the English Channel and arrived safely at our destination.

This voyage being completed, it was now my turn to have a little recreation and rest. I had been with Captain Warren about two years and a half, and was permitted to leave for a month, which I spent amongst friends and relatives in Yorkshire. At the end of this time, Captain Warren's brother, who was the second officer, sent for me to join the *Exmouth* again, bound for Madras and Calcutta, which proposal I gladly accepted. But I was doomed to disappointment. Mr. Warren told me the ship had changed owners, and those to whom it now belonged preferred putting on board their own friends as junior officers, and I was informed that there was no place for me any longer unless I took an inferior position. This I declined. "Disappointments sink the heart of man, but the renewal of hope brings consolation." I received a good testimonial from Captain Warren, and he promised to use his influence in getting me another ship. This happened in a day or two, for a friend of his had just purchased a ship, and was wanting a second officer; I got the captain's name, and was informed he could be found on "'Change" any day. The clerk at the "Jerusalem" Coffee House, which he frequented, gave me the following description of his person: "a tall, thin-faced man, wearing a snuff-coloured coat down to his ankles, his hat turned up a little behind." I said to myself, "I see the man." From this graphic description, I found him next day at the Royal Exchange. There was no time to be lost, and so, although he was in a great crowd, I introduced myself to him as the officer who had sailed with Captain Warren. He looked hard at me for a moment, and then said, " I will take you at the recommendation of your late captain, as second officer; you can join the ship to-morrow, she lies in the London Docks."

I remained in the ship *Hope* (Captain MacCullum) nearly four years, sailing about to the extremities of the commercial world from China to Peru, east and west, wherever the best freights were to be obtained.

I may remark, in passing, that this sudden change of circumstances was calculated to prove a greater benefit to me in after life than if I had remained in an Indiaman. The latter course might be attended with more honour, but the pecuniary advantage would have been less. I had long entertained the idea of getting on, saving money, and buying part of some trading craft with a roving commission to go from port to port in search of some El Dorado out of the common order. This scheme, I imagined, might be realised in the near future, and my youthful fancy pictured it in glowing colours. But alas! long years of service intervened before I attained this object.

CHAPTER VI.

FTER fitting out and taking in a cargo for Singapore, a chief officer being now engaged, we set sail. The *Hope* was about 450 tons burden, her accommodation in the cabin being of the very best order and convenience. An excellent table was provided, with fresh meat and poultry every day, and never during any part of the long voyages do I remember seeing salt beef brought forward. The first officer and I were always the best of friends; he was an excellent seaman and a steady man, though he did not get on so well with the captain, who was a regular martinet. When we fairly got out of the English Channel into, what sailors call, "blue water," he kept all hands on deck the whole of the day, and made the two officers keep a specially good look out at night, he himself being called every four hours. This kind of sailing so close to the wind the chief officer had not been accustomed to, and he purposed leaving the ship at Singapore, when a singular circumstance, which will be narrated hereafter, quite turned him from his purpose. The close drill by night and by day (for I can call it by no other term) seemed to suit me better. I was young, strong, and willing, and thought a few years of it would equip me for any service afloat. Being second officer, I of course kept the captain's watch, and never during the whole time do I remember that he caught me napping. I used to think that he slept with one eye open, for no sooner did the footstep of the officer in charge of the night watches cease to be heard, than he was on deck in an instant. I can answer for myself; he never found the sails out of trim or the ship badly steered, which two points are most important to a vessel propelled entirely by the force of wind.

After crossing the Equator, the captain, who was the owner, and could do as he liked, declared his intention of calling at Cape Town. So we came to an anchor in Table Bay, under the mountain called by this name, which is six thousand feet above the sea. It is as flat as a table, and sometimes there rests on its summit a thin white cloud called " the table cloth." Tourists occasionally are attracted to the top of this mountain to obtain a view of the grand scenery around. This is, however, a dangerous adventure, as fogs frequently set in which last two or three days; there are no guides, and locomotion is arrested for fear of a fall over a steep precipice.

After coming to anchor, the captain went on shore, shortly after which we received a letter from him, ordering the ship to be prepared for a large party of ladies and gentlemen. In a few days they all came on board, accompanied by the captain's bride and her parents —a motley group of Dutch Africaners. The bride was a very elegant person. The marriage had been celebrated during the short stay on shore, and we sailed next morning for Singapore.

We learnt afterwards that the engagement had taken place about six months previously, the manner of which I relate from the lady's own lips. She was walking in the town one day with some friends, when being caught in a shower of rain, they took shelter under a veranda where the gallant captain was lodging. To be brief—it was love at first sight on both sides. For two years they lived happily together, but alas! trouble then came. The captain became a hard drinker, and this may account for all the misery his poor wife experienced; he eventually abandoned wife and child.

Let me here take the opportunity of warning my young readers against this baneful evil, so terrible and soul-destroying in its effects. We have this solemn injunction in God's Word, "Look not thou upon the wine when it is red, when it giveth his colour in the cup, when it moveth itself aright. At the last it biteth like a serpent and stingeth like an adder" (Prov. xxiii., 31-32). These words have been verified in many cases that have come under my notice; clever, gifted men becoming victims to intemperance, and in a few years losing both fortune and character. It is my firm belief that more accidents have happened at sea through intemperance than from any other cause. Here the old adage expresses the mournful truth, "There are more drowned in the wine cup than in the ocean."

We soon discharged our cargo at Singapore. Resenting the captain's very strict discipline, all the sailors ran away from the ship, which was quite the custom, so we exchanged our crew for lascars. Meanwhile we made a voyage to Sumatra, and then back to Singapore. We had on board a super-cargo, and goods to barter with among the Malays for betel-nut, pepper, rattans (cane), and bamboos. The betel - nut resembles a nutmeg in appearance, and is used by the Chinese as a dye. Bamboo is one of the cereal grasses, or a gigantic corn with a ligneous stem, attaining to the height of sixty feet. Once in fifteen years it bears fruit most resembling rice or oats, and then dies like the rest of the cereals. The leaves are abundant, and present to the eye a most elegant appearance; both stems and leaves are of a bright green colour. The houses in this place are built of it chiefly, and the Chinese use it for almost every purpose of furniture. Their ships, as well as masts, sails, and rigging are principally bamboo. The roots of this plant possess a medicinal virtue. The stem is deeply rooted in the ground, and produces a great number of offshoots. These young shoots are sometimes eaten when green, and sometimes made into a preserve with sugar; and last, though not least, the canes from it are used to castigate refractory individuals.

We visited several places for trading, and sometimes the natives came on board in great numbers. The ship was lying at anchor off

Sambelanga, where a small creek of fresh water ran into the sea. One fine evening a party of us went off to enjoy a bath of fresh water, which is always considered a great treat by sailors. It was not until after we had performed our ablutions that we became aware of the fearful risk we had incurred, for we learnt that this part of the river was infested with alligators, and the natives were astonished to see us return in safety. I will mention another narrow escape which we had here. Proceeding further up the creek, we found that it opened out into a lagoon, or lake, on the opposite side of which was a stockade belonging to the party hostile to our trade. As the shades of evening were drawing on it escaped our observation, although we did not pass unnoticed by the Malays, who fired a volley of musketry at us while in the act of landing from our boat. The charge happily passed over our heads, and no one was hurt; but this warning was sufficient to prove to us we were among treacherous natives, and that we must exercise great care if we would escape such ambuscades.

On our landing at another place on the coast called Sewang, we met with better treatment and hospitality. We were regaled with green cocoanuts, drinking the milk out of the shell, a most refreshing beverage, and much like cream, the nut being only imperfectly formed. It was a rare sight to see a man, by means of a simple stirrup or strap, worm himself up like a snake to the top of a tree, fifty feet high, without branches, and cut off some of the nuts, and then return in the same way. Could such a feat be performed in England, what crowds would assemble to witness it!

Sago and sugar are both plentiful here.

Once we entertained a native Rajah of some consequence, who seemed quite a despot, his subjects falling down at his feet and embracing them, as their custom was. He was one day persuaded to dine on board. His manners were not very refined, and he did not quite know how to handle a knife and fork, keeping one of them in each hand, and taking his food in the primitive style—with his fingers. During the dinner hour one of his servants, an Ethiopian, stood at his back with a drawn sword in his hand, keeping guard over his master for fear of treachery; being a treacherous race of men, they suspect all others. In some parts of the Indian Archipelago they are banded together, and prove dangerous enemies to ships in distress as dacoits, ladrones, and pirates. With all this

MALAY PIRATES.

ruffianism about them, strange to say, the Malayan language is the softest and sweetest in the world, and is called the Italian of the East. There is a singular mode of salutation observed by all the Malays; the betel-nut is chewed by them when they meet; a Malay when speaking to any superior must chew his betel, turning it over in his mouth before speaking, as if to digest his suit or petition. The women all chew the betel-nut to make their teeth black, which is supposed to beautify the mouth. I have heard that as the ourang-outang (which some of these people resemble) has very white teeth, they adopt this means to make their teeth black.

We soon loaded the ship and duly arrived at Singapore, where, to our great astonishment, the super-cargo was arrested, taken out of the ship and imprisoned. I may remark here that he had promised the chief officer the command of a ship, but this turned out to be a myth. He must have been a wild speculator, though not with his own money, and belonged to that class who apparently cannot discern between *meum* and *tuum*. In one of his enterprises he purchased the Siamese Twins, when quite young, from their mother—a Chinese who had settled in Siam.

CHAPTER VII.

AFTER settling the dispute with the super-cargo, the chief officer returned on board, and we started for Macao, a Portuguese settlement in China, in the province of Canton. Having discharged the betel-nut and other cargo, we proceeded to Batavia in Java. On our journey thither we had to pass through the Straits of Malacca. These Straits are about six hundred miles long, extending from Singapore to Prince of Wales' Island. The navigation here is safe and the scenery charming—full of the most interesting objects imaginable, such as any tourist would delight to visit and enjoy.

About the middle of this Malay Peninsula stands the ancient city of Malacca, opposite to which rises in bold relief the Golden Mountain, and the far-famed Mount Ophir. Many stories are related about this part of the world, which by some has been supposed to be the Golden Chersonese of the ancients. The Queen of

Sheba is said to have sent ships to load here with the gold, precious stones, and spices she gave to King Solomon. This may be partly true and partly legendary, as there are no fewer than five places which claim the honour of being the Ophir of the Bible.

In the city and neighbourhood of Malacca are found many ancient ruins, some having the appearance of pyramids, and others of large castles and fortifications. That the historic account is the true one, I entertain but little doubt, confirmed as it is by the fact that wild peacocks, apes, and spices abound there to a large extent.

I must not omit to mention the delicious fruits so plentiful in these parts, the pineapple is the finest and best in the world ; the mangosteen, queen of fruits, very delicious, having a flavour of mango, pomegranate and orange ; cocoanuts in abundance, the shells of which will contain an English quart ; the durain, or bread-fruit, which, though it has not a pleasant smell, has yet a delightful taste, and contains about a dozen large seeds, the size of a sweet chestnut, capable of being made into bread ; besides all other tropical fruits, such as mangoes, bananas, custard apples, alligator pears, guavas, lemons, oranges, etc.

Here I must briefly allude to a branch of
the human family, the most remarkable, in my
opinion, on the face of the earth. Entirely
separated from all others, they live in trees,
and unlike every other savage tribe, they never
change their habitation. They remind me of
the inhabitants of the lake-dwellings of pre-
historic times. They refuse all intercourse with
strangers, and are compelled to adopt this
mode of life on account of the numbers of
tigers infesting their woods. I was told by
some one who had visited them, that they tie
monkeys to their trees, fatten them, kill them,
and live upon them. They have no language,
but on the appearance of a stranger, they set
up, one and all, a hideous chattering, which
soon drives the intruder away. Miss Isabella
Bird (afterwards Mrs. Bishop), gives a full
account of these Melanesians, whose name I
have forgotten.

I have passed up and down these Straits five
times, their average width is twenty-five miles,
and they are seldom, if ever, visited by gales
of wind, but there are heavy squalls lasting
about three hours, of such a terrific character,
that it is impossible to carry a stitch of canvas,
all the sails have to be clued up and furled
very tightly. But the goodness of God has

provided an unerring warning of the approaching storm ; a small dark cloud, not bigger than a man's hand, appears in the horizon off Sumatra ; by and bye it assumes the form of a dark arch, then quickly bursts upon the ship with a tremendous fall of rain, accompanied by thunder and lightning, the forked lightning playing all round the ship and lighting up the prevailing darkness. At the expiration of about three hours, the winds cease, and the air is balmy and pleasant. These storms almost always come on at midnight and leave a phosphorescent light at the three mast heads, and every yard arm, the whole atmosphere being so charged with electricity. These bright lights resemble the "Ignis fatuus," sometimes called "Will-o'-the-wisp," which is seen in marshy grounds at home. While, on one occasion, we were admiring this strange phenomenon, I remember sending a boy up to fetch the lantern down on deck, but recollecting it might give him an electric shock, I called him down before he reached the top.

Before leaving China we again changed our crew, this time from lascars to English sailors. While the Asiatics were on board, I had an opportunity of learning to speak Hindustani, which proved to me in after life a most valuable acquisition—being engaged in the Indian trade for several years. After threading our passage amongst the many islands of these Straits into the Indian Ocean, we finally arrived at Batavia, the capital of Java, and of the Dutch East Indies. The air here is very unwholesome, and is represented by James Cook as the grave of European navigators. We lost five or six of the sailors during our stay, and the remainder went to the hospital. Those who died on the ship were taken out to sea and thrown overboard without any service being read over them, like so many dead dogs, for the authorities would not allow them to be buried on shore. About three miles out from the harbour was a bar which was very much infested with crocodiles of enormous size, some from ten to fifteen feet in length, which doubtless fed upon the dead bodies of our crew.

The captain never once visited the ship during her loading, he and his wife were living high up in the interior, where the hills were considered as healthy as any part of the globe. In fact the temple of Hygiene might be erected there. I was, myself, all but carried off by this malarious climate ; as a proof, I remember the old cook saying to me one day, referring to this time, "First you turned white, then yellow, then a little greenish, and I predicted you would never come out of your cabin again alive." The doctor, who was Dutch, was sent on board to attend the chief officer; he was lying quite prostrate in his cabin, and remained in that condition many weeks. I showed him the sick patients, pretending to have nothing much amiss with myself, and determined to brave it out with exercise and work. I must add that in addition to this malarious atmosphere, the thermometer sometimes registered forty degrees difference between noon and midnight. The suddenness of death was so frightful that I inquired of the doctor what was the cause. He replied, "Epilepsy." I can only say that my escape must have been .owing to the great goodness of God; besides this, my invariable moderation was doubtless in my favour.

Finally, having completed the lading of the ship with a cargo of sugar, we sailed away from this noxious climate. But the attack of illness left me with a fever and ague which continued more or less troublesome and weakening until we once more reached the Cape of Good Hope, and the consummation

F

of my hopes. We had no medicine on board; therefore, immediately on arriving, I sent a man off for some quinine pills, which acted like magic—quinine being a specific for ague.

Here I must relate another painful story. The captain and his wife went on shore, leaving to me the entire management of the ship, with instructions to send the sick to the hospital at Cape Town. Among them was the chief officer, who had been confined to his cabin during the five weeks' passage from Java, and who, sad to relate, during our short stay here breathed his last, his strength being completely exhausted. He was a superior seaman, as before noted, and a man of robust constitution. But alas! how frequently it happens that the strongest succumb to the deadly influences of malaria and miasma, while those apparently less healthy survive.

We remained a week, and then with fresh hands on board proceeded homewards, the captain, myself, and a youngster alone remaining out of the crew who left England on the outward voyage to Singapore. It appeared by the charter we were to call at Falmouth for orders where to discharge the cargo, but our destination turned out to be Rotterdam, so we sailed up the English Channel, through the

Straits of Dover into the North Sea, and arrived at Helvoetsluys, and then came into the Maese River, where the fine, rich, and well-built town stands. This was the route taken by George the Third, on his way to Hanover. It is said when he breakfasted at Helvoetsluys, the landlord charged his Majesty sixpence each for eggs. The king thought it an imposition, and complained, remarking that eggs were not so scarce there; to which the man replied, "Your Majesty, eggs are not scarce, but kings are." This incident shows that George the Third was no stranger to habits of frugality.

CHAPTER VIII.

AFTER discharging the cargo of sugar at Rotterdam, our next trip was up the Baltic to St. Petersburg. Compared with our former long voyages, this short trip was more like a pleasant cruise in a yacht: being summer time we had perpetual daylight nearly all the voyage. Passing through into the North Sea again, we made for the Kattegat, a gulf which divides Norway from Denmark, and by which the Northern Ocean communicates with the Baltic or East Sea. Passing along, we came to Elsinore, where stands a castle that is also a fortress, in which it is said Shakespeare wrote his tragedy of Hamlet. When Admiral Nelson sailed through this Strait, called the Sound, on his way to bombard Copenhagen, he fired several shots into the fortification, some of which were collected and kept to show visitors; these they call an "English Welcome!" We came

A WESTERLY GALE IN THE NORTH ATLANTIC.

to anchor here to take a pilot on board, who, with myself, navigated the ship to St. Petersburg, at the top of the great gulf of Finland.

The captain entrusted me with the entire management of the ship as commanding officer, which position I occupied throughout the voyage, he himself remaining on shore during the lading and unlading of the cargo.

We passed the city of Copenhagen, one of the most uniform and best built cities in the North. It owes its present noble appearance to a great fire which broke out in 1728, destroying five churches and sixty-seven streets, many of them narrow and ill-shaped. It has since been rebuilt in a better style, and a few only of the wooden houses remain. Its appearance from the sea is strikingly beautiful. Nearly opposite stands a small islet with an observatory, on which Tycho Brahe, the Danish astronomer lived. On our homeward voyage, passing out through the Sound towards Gothenburg, a famous town in Sweden, with a splendid harbour, situated at the mouth of the river Gotha, we leave the calm smooth Baltic, with its still, tideless waters, and enter into the North Atlantic Ocean, where the westerly gales in the winter season are most terrific to encounter, one of which I remember some forty-five years ago. In the autumn, when the ships are leaving the Baltic ports, they are sometimes caught by these heavy storms and gales and obliged to bear up for a port in Norway. The Norwegian pilots are always on the look-out in stormy weather to pilot these ships into some of the safe fiords so numerous on this otherwise dangerous coast. Assistance is usually rendered in the following fashion. A man and woman come off through a stormy sea in a small dingey, which is only capable of carrying two persons. It is impossible to come too near the ship, as the smallest collision would prove fatal to the boat. How, then, do they manage it? Ah! there's the rub! From the ship is thrown into the boat a rope with a running bowline knot, the woman passes it round her waist, throws herself overboard, and is taken into the ship as pilot, for she knows where to anchor in safety. The man takes the dingey back, which the woman could only manage alone with the utmost risk and difficulty. All this is done to earn the paltry sum of a few gilders! An act of the most daring .bravery on the part of what is usually called, the "softer sex"! Hear this, ye young gentlemen of England who live at home at ease!

Being the summer season we did not require
any such pilot, but proceeded towards the
Pentland Firth, between the Orkney Islands
and Scotland, passing by John o' Groats'
House, the *ultima thule* of Great Britain. We
then sailed through the North Channel of the
Irish Sea, and arrived safely in Liverpool.
This concludes a voyage of two years, fraught
with many stirring incidents and narrow
escapes, the details of which I pass over.
How much this calls for thankfulness to the
Divine Providence! "He maketh the storm
a calm so that the waves thereof are still.
Then are they glad because they be quiet; so
He bringeth them unto their desired haven."

I do not remember being absent from duty
more than one day during this voyage, and
now thought it time to take a little relaxa-
tion. We delivered the cargo in the Princes'
Dock, Liverpool, and I then proceeded
homewards. After spending a month in
Yorkshire, I returned to the ship again; she
was chartered to take out a cargo to Lima,
in South America, and she lay in the Liverpool
docks about four months. I remained on
board with only two or three men, as the
cargo came in very slowly; this was a rest
from the toils of a sea voyage.

CHAPTER IX.

FTER setting sail, I have to record a most tedious passage of nearly six months before finally arriving at Lima. This, however, was in great measure relieved by the society of four passengers, a lady and her three daughters, the two elder of whom were highly accomplished in music and languages.

We had on board a Highland crew from Oban, the captain's native place, with a piper. in full costume, but I am happy to say his bagpipes produced no discord, although the ladies and myself, being English, greatly preferred the dulcet notes of the guitar and the human voice to the melancholy droning of his instrument. For the most part the weather was exceedingly boisterous, with excessive rain. The old lady and her three daughters, unfortunately for them, were not on good terms with the captain. I remember, when off Cape Horn, a small island south of

Terra del Fuego, they said to me, " Will this voyage ever terminate, do you think? We have passed twenty-four Sabbaths on board, and it seems longer than the whole of our lifetime." I endeavoured to cheer them up by the assurance that when we were fairly round the Cape on the west coast we should get into the south-east trade winds, and soon forget all our troubles, doubts, and fears.

I may mention here that we passed near Juan Fernandez, an island off the west coast of Chili, rendered famous by Defoe having founded his story of the life and adventures of Robinson Crusoe on the solitary residence there of Alexander Selkirk (formerly coxswain to Dampier) for above four years.

I got the first glimpse of the Andes at a distance of one hundred and twenty miles, and called the ladies up to see the welcome sight. Very soon we arrived at Callao, the seaport for Lima, a consummation to be devoutly thankful for after our long and tedious voyage. The harbour is spacious; the best in the whole State of Peru. It is formed by the island of San Lorenzo, the narrow passage between it and the mainland being called the Boqueron Channel. This is noted for one of the most daring actions ever per-

formed by any captain in the English Navy.
A Spanish corvette, a vessel smaller than a
frigate, was lying in the roads off Callao.
Lord Cochrane commanded an English sloop
of war, half the size of the corvette in tonnage,
men and guns.   Cochrane's ship crept up the
Boqueron   passage,   and   came   to   anchor.
Having manned his launch with a crew of
daring fellows like himself, shortly after
midnight, they rowed round the corvette, and
finding all the sentries asleep, climbed up
the chains of the fore-rigging, muzzled the
sleeping sentries, nailed fast the cabin doors,
battened down the hatches, slipped the cable,
and towed the Spaniard alongside of the
English ship as a prize, without spilling a
drop of blood !

Our ship had been reported the evening
before our arrival.   The following morning,
Mr. Goodfellow, the husband and father of
the lady passengers, came on board; they
were all in high glee, and, as I had predicted, appeared to have forgotten all their
former troubles.   While our cargo was being
discharged, which occupied about three weeks,
I visited the family at their residence in the
capital, Lima, situated nearly six miles from
Callao.   I remember on one occasion, dining

with them at the house of a friend, who provided a sumptuous banquet, regaling us abundantly with all the fruits of the country. Some of the guests were Americans, and, singularly enough, a Mr. Longfellow was present, and four Goodfellows, father, mother, and daughters.

This caused great amusement amongst the young people, who told me the following story of the American gentleman. When he joined the United States frigate, *Brautewein*, as purser, under the command of Commodore Reid, an order was given to make two cots, one for the commodore and the other for the purser, with the remark that the commodore was a very tall man (he was six feet two inches), nothing being said about the stature of the purser, Mr. Longfellow. The sailmaker made his cot one foot longer than that for the commodore, but as Mr. Longfellow was in reality a very little fellow, the mistake was the cause of much merriment.

In the course of the evening Mrs. Goodfellow confided to me the great secret that both her daughters were engaged to be married to wealthy English merchants residing at Lima. The marriages took place, and

I afterwards heard that both proved to be happy and prosperous. This sudden change of circumstances reinstated them in their former position, which they had lost for a time through their father's indiscretion.

We could understand how acceptable was the English element in Lima, when we learned that the ladies residing there (half-bred Spaniards) were much addicted to pleasure and vanity. They were remarkable for their beauty, and especially for the smallness of their feet, submitting readily to the amputation of their small toes in order to narrow their feet; one doctor, it is said, having made a small fortune by this practice. The mothers, unwilling to be thought old, are addressed by their daughters as "sister." The priests here, I was told, were intriguing to an extent scarcely credible, and there is one to every fifty of the population. When they can no longer squeeze more gifts out of the old ladies, they tell them to post a letter to the Virgin Mary with money in it—an arrangement which the postman understands very well!

Some of my readers may remember the terrible catastrophe which occured at Santiago more than twenty years ago. A service

of three days and three nights was being
held in one of the cathedrals, and the whole
building was lighted with candles and highly
ornamented. Suddenly a cry of "Fire!" was
raised; a fearful panic ensued, and the con-
gregation fled to the doors, all of which un-
ortunately opened inwards; consequently many
persons were crushed to death. The priests,
with characteristic selfishness, never offered
any assistance. They were in the sacristy
and escaped. About three hundred and fifty
charred bodies were found, many of them
standing in the attitude of prayer.

There are no buildings in Lima of more
than two stories high, owing to the dread of
earthquakes, with which the city has been so
often visited. Callao was once swallowed up
by a terrible earthquake, the sea afterwards
rushing into the town, and overwhelming all
the houses and inhabitants, one man only
being saved in a boat to tell the tale.

Peru is rich in minerals, especially silver.
During the time when it acknowledged the
sovereignty of Spain, a Viceroy, on one
occasion, was sent out, who was received
with great . honour and pomp; one of the
streets leading to the palace being paved
with ingots of silver. But alas! this apparent

loyalty was of short duration; the country soon after proclaimed her independence of Spain, and the same streets were changed into scenes of strife and bloodshed. The Peruvians remained in this state of rebellion and anarchy for four years or more—continually changing their President. It was said they all knew how to conjugate the verb to shoot, I shoot, thou shootest, we shoot, they shoot; recklessness of human life seeming to characterize those men to whom dangers are most frequent and imminent.

I remember experiencing the shock of an earthquake at Santa. As for describing the sensation produced by an event so unusual to me, I will not make the attempt, but leave it to the reader's imagination.

CHAPTER X.

WE completed our loading at Peyta, a beautiful little bay, but destitute of fresh water. The Springs were at a distance of three miles from the harbour; a supply of water was conveyed by donkeys in calabashes, or dried gourds, consequently it was very scarce, and dearer than spirits. There are numbers of pariah dogs here in the streets, which nobody owns, acting the part of scavengers. About mid-day they usually assembled and set up a frightful howling for water; failing to obtain which they rushed off to the Springs.

Having taken our scanty supply of water for the homeward passage, and before finally leaving the coast, we came to an anchor one night in a bay off Arequipa, to take in a quantity of silver ore. In order to evade the Custom House duties, a proceeding which I cannot justify, a signal was given by showing certain lights, after seeing which, from the

G

shore, there came off in a boat three Spaniards, armed with pistols and daggers, swarthy, fierce-looking fellows. It appeared they had conveyed two tons of silver packed in ceroons, or skins of bullocks, for convenience of carriage on mules, over the mountain passes, travelling only by night, to avoid the bandits. We were avoiding the Custom duties, they, the robbers. I counted forty packages containing a hundredweight each of silver nuggets; these were carefully stowed under the main hatches, and those terrible looking fellows went on shore. Our freight being now complete, gladly enough we sailed away, to run down the south-east trade winds and get into the "Variables." It was the winter season when we arrived off Cape Horn. The storms and snow-squalls we met with were most severe and dangerous; we saw the wreck of a ship, bottom upwards. The days were very short, for the sun appeared at nine o'clock and set at three, rising no higher at mid-day than it looks at midnight in the Arctic circle in summer. Eighteen hours of darkness made the night watches very tedious. One night I had the middle watch below, but could not sleep. I was called at four a.m. to my duties, and found to my dismay the snow had made its way to my bed, and was partly frozen to

ANSWERING THE SIGNAL FROM THE SHIP.

the mattress. We at last weathered this in-
hospitable region, where these heavy seas and
gales exceeded in severity all those I have
ever encountered in my other voyages. The
rest of our passage to Liverpool lasted about
ninety days, during the whole of which time
we were on short allowance of water.

Our next voyage was to Hobart Town, Tasmania, and then Sydney, New South Wales.
I will not dwell upon this part of my story,
but will take my readers to Calcutta, where
we safely arrived *en route* to the Antipodes.
Whilst at Calcutta I had the honour of
dining with one of the sons of Tippoo Saib,
the Sultan of Seringapatam, who, after the
siege of that place in 1799 had been given to
the English General as an hostage, with his
brother, when they were both quite young.
The Prince was very black, he wore the sable
livery of the burning sun, but in manner he
was as gentle as a lamb. From this port
we sailed to the Isle of France with a cargo
of rice, and returning again to Calcutta, I
left this ship on my own account. The
captain became such a hard drinker I was
afraid to stay any longer with him. On thus
summarily leaving the *Hope* and Captain
M———, with whom I remained nearly four

years, of course all my cherished hopes of advancement suddenly collapsed. The last account I heard of him and the ship, was that the men and officers refused to proceed with him any further than Kidderpore (which is one mile from Calcutta) although she was bound for Sydney, New South Wales, all of them being in a mutinous state, I believe. I heard also that the captain had deserted his wife and child, sending her a broken ring and a farewell for ever. I removed all my traps to the next ship in the tier—the *Pegasus*, and went to the Isle of France; and then again to the same place in the ship *Cavendish Bentinck*, making three voyages to the same port and back to Calcutta.

In thus leaving the *Hope* and joining the *Cavendish Bentinck*, I had what sailors call "an Irish rise," becoming second officer after being for a time commanding officer. In the *Cavendish Bentinck*, which was called a "country walla" (or ship), we took about two hundred coolies to work the sugar plantations. This was after the manumission of slaves. Most of these men were kidnapped by the Sircars and Ghaut Serangs in India; they were first drugged and then put on board in that state. Some of them on regaining consciousness, and perceiving how they had been duped, were with great difficulty restrained from jumping overboard into the river Hooghly.

The climate of the Mauritius is very fine. Here is shewn the tomb of the two eccentric lovers, Paul and Virginia. Having visited this island three times, I had ample opportunity of seeing its many beauties, amongst them the remarkable Peter Botte, three thousand feet high, capped by overhanging rocks.

Some very curious stories are told with reference to the observatory here for signalling ships in the offing about to arrive in Port Lewis — which is the only harbour in this island,—and a M. Pepigné, who had charge of it. It has been confidently affirmed that he has seen and reported vessels at sea one hundred and fifty miles distant from the island. On one occasion he warned the French authorities of the approach of an English squadron of war ships coming to take the place by storm. This caution was totally disregarded, but the English nevertheless did come and take possession. Other cases of the mirage—for that was the explanation of this incident—occurred in which M. Pepigné had seen vessels dismasted at sea, making for this port, two or three days before their arrival. Most sailors have heard the story of " the Flying Dutchman," off the Cape of Good Hope, carrying a press of canvas lower and aloft, when other ships almost in the immediate neighbourhood were under close reefed top-sails. I entertain no doubt as to the truth of these stories, although one does not hear of such things in our days. The Frenchman affirmed that he only saw these objects during a particular state of the atmosphere. He made a great secret of it, and persistently refused to impart it to any one.

I have witnessed many strange mirages on the African Coast, such as are seen in the desert, and have also read of the Spectre of the Brocken, seen in some part of Germany, where it appeared that a cavalry regiment was going through all the evolutions and movements of a body of troops on a morass that would not bear the weight of one single soldier. Although it does not belong to this narrative, I cannot forbear, while on the subject of mirages or optical illusions, recording what I once saw when staying in a romantic part of North Wales. One midsummer evening as I wandered out from the village, which is situated in a glen between two mountain ridges,

I was suddenly surprised by a most beautiful picture of a bay of the sea, much resembling the bay of Naples. I at once concluded it was a mirage. On the right was an abrupt termination of the mountain opposite the one on which I stood; on the left a dark serrated cumulus, with a small detached cloud, having the appearance of a rocky islet, such as is often seen at the extremity of headlands. The whole scene was marvellously beautiful, and quite natural to the eye of a nautical man. There it lay before me looking like a sea of glass, which seemed to merge into the bright sky of the north-west horizon, where daylight had scarcely faded before the setting sun. While thus musing, and as if to make the picture complete, I heard the sound of running brooks and murmuring streams. Below the mountain gorge was a cataract which sounded like the sea gently heaving up from its placid bosom the smallest wavelets on a shingly beach.

But to return to Port Lewis. Whilst there, I saw a remarkable specimen of the cocoanut from the Seychelle Islands, found in no other part of the world. It is much larger than the common kind, its shell being a bi-valve, and sometimes it is found with its roots in the sea, but it flourishes even in that state.

The peculiarity of this cocoanut is that while it bears flowers like all nut trees, the sap seems to exude from the flower and to flow into the bi-valve shell, and as it comes to maturity the shell closes, and a large kernel is formed.

The Seychelle Islands lie low, being formed by the action of myriads of infusoria or microscopic insects, elaborating the white coral rock from ingredients in the sea-water alone. They have been known in the short space of a few months to build up a coral reef of considerable height above the surface. In tropical seas there is always a large quantity of vegetable *débris* floating about, and in this marvellous manner islands are formed, and vegetation quickly springs up.

The Dutch, who professed to have at one time the monopoly of the islands producing spices, built a plantation here, and cultivated them largely; but at last, fearing they might fall into the hands of the English, burned it up.

On our arrival at Calcutta in the *Cavendish Bentinck*, I went on shore to live, and took such a liking to the place, and the mode of life there, with its many comforts and numerous servants, that I almost made up

my mind to settle in India, for a time at
least. I used to go with friends on excursions
up and down the river in rowing boats with
six men, towing another boat for cooking
purposes. Sometimes we went long distances,
to Barrackpoor and Chinsura, and even beyond, to Chandernagore, a French settlement.
At Chinsura I found that the chaplain, the
Rev. J. H. A. Rudd, was an old school-
fellow of mine; he had settled out there,
and his wife and family were with him.
About two hundred and forty miles up the
river Ganges, the rainfall is sometimes
registered as much as fifteen feet per annum,
at Chera Poonje. My brother, who was for
seventeen years officer and commander in
the East India Company's steamers, told me
he had seen the rivers so swollen with the
rains as to rise to the height of fifteen feet
of water, when, in the dry season their
ordinary height was only three feet. On one
of our trips on the Hooghly to the Botanical
Gardens, we were shewn the great Banyan
Tree, the most remarkable feature of which is
the property it possesses of throwing out
supports from its horizontal branches, which
take root as soon as they reach the ground.
Here all the spice-bearing trees, gum trees,

and others of medicinal virtue are found and cultivated with the greatest care, amongst others the Cinchona or Jesuit's bark, from which quinine is extracted. It is a remarkable fact in connection with the Cinchona (a species of laurel) that the bark which contains the drug may be stripped off without killing the tree. The latter is plastered and bandaged up very carefully after the operation; a new bark then forms, and in this manner the tree is preserved from destruction.

CHAPTER XI.

I SOON grew weary of this idleness, however, and determined to accept the first offer of a situation for another voyage. I had not long to wait, for Captain Bennett, who had only a day or two before been appointed to the command of the *Heroine*, offered me the post of second officer. The chief officer, with his wife and child, lived on board as ship-keeper. They were all hard drinkers; I have even seen the child, only ten years old, so intoxicated as to be more dead than alive. I never saw the mother, but from all accounts she was as intemperate as her husband, and, as may be imagined, everything on board was in a wretched state of disorder. I found Captain Bennett a kind-hearted man, and soon gained his full confidence, being entrusted in his absence with the duty of getting ready for the voyage, and of taking in the bales of cotton for China. We lived on board, as the custom was, all the time of loading, the captain only visiting the ship once a day.

With a cargo of six thousand bales of cotton, and six passengers, we sailed for Singapore and China. I had been suffering somewhat from over-work during the ship's outfit, but the balmy breezes and a day's shooting on the Prince of Wales' Island, restored me to perfect health. Our course lay through the Straits of Malacca again. Nothing of any particular note took place until our arrival within the Straits. The captain, being extremely delicate, left the entire management of the ship to his officers. The chief officer took advantage of this to indulge more freely than ever in his brandy. As an instance of his carelessness, he one fine day fell asleep, and allowed the ship to get ashore. I awoke him, then called the captain, and told him the state of affairs. He was very unwell at the time, and the passengers were much alarmed. My position as second officer was on the top-gallant forecastle. He called out and enquired what I was going to do, seeming utterly dazed and bewildered as he gave the command, " Let go the anchor." To this I objected, saying, if the anchor was cast, it might go through the ship's forefoot. He then asked what I proposed to do, to which I replied, " If you leave it to me I will soon get her afloat again," which I did in the space of half-an-hour. This happened near the dinner-hour, and when I entered the cabin the passengers met me with a courteous greeting, and warm thanks, declaring I had saved their lives; at any rate their fears were allayed, and the ship received no injury, but had she struck on a coral reef instead of grounding on mud, the consequences might have been fatal.

Two days after, the chief officer had charge of the watch, from six to eight, which is called the "dog watch." It was very dark when I heard a man on the look-out exclaim, "A ship right ahead close to!" Rushing forward with a night telescope I found it was the Round Arrow, a small rock in the centre of the Straits; our course was immediately altered, and we escaped the danger. It proved that he had altered the ship's course two points of the compass. When remonstrated with for so doing, I well remember his reply: "If you are anxious to avoid a rock or shoal, steer for it, and you will be sure to miss it"—a species of logic I have never yet comprehended. In two days more we came to anchor off Singapore, when Captain Bennett, with the passengers, left the ship. About eventide a boat came off with two letters from the captain, one to the chief officer, and one to myself, the latter asking me to take full charge as chief officer. The purport of the other was to dismiss the man who had committed such egregious blunders through drink.

His dismissal had the effect of sobering him down at once, and he, with his daughter, cleared out next morning as sober as a judge. The following day the captain came on board, when I told him everything was done according to his orders. But we were minus a second officer to take my place, and were unable to find one. Here I could foresee a grave responsibility resting upon me, but the ship being well manned in other respects, I at once consented to go on as we were, with the understanding that the second mate's pay should be divided between the captain and myself.

The south-west monsoon was blowing in the China Sea, in consequence of which our course lay through the Java Sea, with its ten thousand islands and intricate navigation. We sailed through the eastern passage, between the Philippine Islands and Borneo, Celebes and the Spice Islands, into the Pacific Ocean, passing the Pelew islands.

I distinctly remember one morning when we were drawing near to the Hen and Chickens, a coral bank in the midst of these Straits, I came on deck, and found the darkest fog prevailing I ever saw. The captain was so extremely unwell as to be unable to leave his state-room. In this emergency—but for a moment only—I began to tremble, feeling the serious responsibility of the situation. Suddenly it flashed into my mind to mount up to the top-mast head, and there to my delight and surprise the sun was shining in full splendour, proving the truth of those cheering words, "There is a silver lining to every dark cloud." There I remained, but only for a few moments; compared with those on deck, I was in the serene atmosphere of heaven, being for a short time above the clouds. A tropical sun was shining in all its brilliancy, every object sparkling with beauty. I could see the cocoa-nut and palm trees and lofty foliage apparently half-a-mile distant, while the ship was gliding slowly through the dense fog, stem-on towards the rocks. There was no time, however, for reflection, still many serious thoughts rushed into my mind; above all, heartfelt thanksgiving for our preservation from disaster. I at once altered the course of the ship's head, before coming down from aloft. The low fog by which we were surrounded continued two hours longer, and at mid-day it was perfectly clear and bright. Sometimes the fog lifts itself up and disappears in a mysterious way. It is seen to be thin in some parts and thick in others, rolling itself up into bales not unlike

H

snowballs, then it suddenly vanishes and all is clear. I have often seen this in Newfoundland and Nova Scotia. The natives call the light breezes which cause these movements of the mist, " fog-eaters."

Immediately after this another sight presented itself, such as I had never before witnessed. There was no wind on deck, but a light air aloft kept the upper sails sleeping, while not a ripple stirred the surface of the water. We were sailing slowly over a sea as clear as crystal, and we could distinctly mark out every feature of the submerged coral bank. It was like a city of palaces, with lofty pinnacles, spacious chambers, and wide terraces, while seaweed of various hues clothed all in lovely colours. We sounded in nine fathoms, and at the next cast found no bottom at sixty fathoms, On reviewing our safe passage through the Straits, I could only feel the deepest gratitude for our preservation from harm, for the loss of the ship here would probably have been fatal to us all even in the finest weather. In the first place, the coast is infested with Malay pirates who would have attacked us the moment they perceived the ship was disabled; besides which, to sleep on the shore one night in the bush would most likely have caused our deaths. What is termed the upas, or poison-tree of Java, so notorious for its malarious effect on all animal life, is common here.

THE BASHEES.

That it has poisonous secretions is a fact, but that the atmosphere surrounding it is dele-terious is entirely fabulous. I have no doubt

that this notion has arisen from the fact that
under the branches of the tamarind tree which
abounds here, a quantity of carbonic acid gas
accumulates at night time, and causes death to
any one sleeping under its shade.

Pursuing our course into the Pacific, we
entered the China Sea by the Bashees, between
Luzon and Manilla; the Bashees being a
cluster of rocky islands. One of these. islets
is a burning mountain, we saw it while active,
emitting volumes of smoke. We then came
to Macao, where Captain Bennett was obliged
to be left to consult a medical man. I then
had sole charge of the ship during the remainder
of the voyage till she cast anchor at Whampoo,
and was the only white man among this miscellaneous crew. Whampoo being the part
of the river nearest to Canton was the most
convenient spot to discharge the cotton bales.
After passing the Bocca Tigris, the narrowest
part of the river, a boat came to meet us,
and to my surprise we found that the owner
of the *Heroine* was in the boat. He asked
me where Captain Bennett was. I said he
was left at Macao. He then enquired for the
chief officer. I replied he was left ashore at
Singapore. Then he asked who I was. I
told him I joined the ship at Calcutta as

second officer. He appeared much surprised to see me, an entire stranger to himself, in full command of one of his ships. After remaining some time on board, and satisfying himself and his friend who accompanied him, that the officer left in charge was worthy of his entire confidence judging from the way in which the ship and crew were commanded, he left, and we sailed up to the anchorage. The next morning the China "chops" or cargo boats came alongside and we commenced discharging. I had to take an account, single-handed, of the weight of every bale of cotton, there being no other European in the ship.

CHAPTER XII.

AFTER the cargo was discharged the captain, who was slightly better, rejoined his ship, when we left Whampoo for the Typa, a safe anchorage two miles from Macao; the owner, Mr. R——, came to live on board.

At this time the Chinese Opium War broke out, and all the trade between the English shipowners and China merchants suddenly collapsed. In consequence of this, our owner fell into a very desponding state; moreover, the captain, for whom I felt the deepest sympathy, was compelled to resign his post on account of continued ill-health.

Just before this an event occurred which I shall have cause, indeed, to remember with thankfulness as long as I live. Once more, through "the good hand of my God upon me," I was saved from a violent death. The details of this incident I now proceed to relate. To my great surprise, I was awakened

one morning at daylight by the gunner, who
was much excited, informing me that the
crew were in a mutinous state, armed with
sticks and bamboos, and intending to make
an attack upon the ship and officers. I at
once called the captain, the owner, and an
American captain, who most fortunately was
sleeping on board that night. I had persuaded him to take a " shake-down " on board,
in preference to returning to his own ship, as
the night was so very dark, and his presence
amongst us proved of the utmost service in
this extremity. The mutineers were three to
one that we could muster on our side.
Having armed myself with a cutlass, the
first sight that met my eye was the captain
lying helpless on the main deck with one of
the strongest amongst the ringleaders kneeling
upon his chest. Seeing me armed with a
sword, the rascal bolted under the forecastle
and disappeared, having jumped into the sea,
as I supposed, out of the port-hole. I then
went round to the other side of the main-
deck with the American captain to charge the
rest of the men who had ranged themselves
five feet above our heads on the top-gallant
forecastle. One fellow, with well-directed aim,
hurled a missile at me (twenty pounds weight),

knowing that could I be got rid of they would have it all their own way. To avoid this, I slipped aside, and received a sliding blow on the head which made a scalp wound, the scar of which remains to this day. When the fellows saw their attempt had failed, and while we were mounting up the ladder, three or four of the leaders jumped overboard and swam to the shore, the rest gave way, and the mutiny was quelled.

The ship was lying in the Typa, about two miles from Macao, and within half a mile from the shore. While my wound was being dressed the runaways were seen climbing up the beach. They contrived to get to Macao, where they had the audacity to consult the Portuguese authorities, and summon the owner for their wages and a passage back to Calcutta. I went with the other witnesses to report their mutinous conduct ; the plaintiffs were not only non-suited but imprisoned, some for three, some for six months, with hard labour. These men, notwithstanding their shameful behaviour, were entitled to some sympathy, for they had been wronged. Had they, instead of resorting to these violent measures, applied for redress to the authorities on shore, they could have legally claimed their wages and a passage back to Calcutta.

I was now left on board alone, with only the fragments of a crew, to ruminate on the situation, which I did with some feelings of dissatisfaction, as this serious scrimmage, which might have cost me my life, had been occasioned by the owner deliberately breaking a legal contract made by Captain Bennett in Calcutta, that the lascars should be taken back to the port of their embarkation. I have always considered a contract to be a solemn engagement, binding on both parties, and woe betide the man who breaks it !

Meanwhile, a letter came from the owner offering me the command of the *Heroine*. For three days I hesitated before accepting this post, but my old dread of being un-employed haunting me again and again, I at length agreed to take it.

About this time we were much harassed by the Chinese Government, and were obliged constantly to move about from port to port at the entrance of the river, sometimes lying at Tong Roo Cap Sing Moon, Cum Sing Moon, till we settled down finally at Hong Kong, one of the safest and most spacious harbours in the world. The town, at that time, consisted of only a few huts inhabited by fishermen. Here we lay at anchor for nearly three years, engaged in transmitting merchandise from ships to the shore. Several English and American merchants being driven out of Canton, came to live on board. Commissioner Lin, who came from Pekin, ordered all the opium in the ships trading in that nefarious traffic to be given up and burned.

At this critical juncture, who should turn up, to my great surprise, but my brother Tom! Our meeting here was brought about in a similar way to that in which we had met years before in London. A man came up to me and said, "Sir, I have seen your brother, he is in the fleet." "Impossible!" I replied, "my brother is in America!" "He must be your brother, for you are as much alike as two peas!" I hastened to his ship, and true enough, there was my brother Tom! but bronzed and altered during the five years we had not seen each other. He was then commanding officer of the Bombay ship, *Ruperelle*, belonging to a Parsee, whereas I had always considered him captain of the *Mary Anne*, sailing between St. John's, New Brunswick, and Liverpool. As I was then in need of a chief officer, he came to me in the *Heroine*; the elder brother serving the younger. Another instance of an Irish rise, this time in *his* case, not *mine*.

The typhoons or hurricanes in China are very dangerous to navigation, and ships were continually arriving at Hong Kong in a leaky state. As there were no docks for repairs, we received their cargo on board the *Heroine* during repairs and reloading. My brother complained of the owner of the ship interfering with him in his duty, and soon left, taking a passage for Calcutta, where he remained seventeen years in the East India Company's service in command of a steamer.

Let me here mention a curious custom in operation at this time. On the arrival of a ship, the Chinese put on board the following notice in English :—" Should any accident happen and a Chinese coolie or labourer be killed by the fall of any chest or bale while discharging or taking in cargo, a European or Fau Qui (white devil) must forfeit his life in lieu thereof." Upon one occasion a Chinaman was killed by a box, which, slipping out of the slings, fell upon and crushed him. This caused a great commotion, and the news being told at once to the mandarins, they ordered the trade with all the English ships to be instantly suspended. The loss occa-

sioned by this command, had it continued,
would have been enormous, as many ships,
some 1,400 tons burden, were loading there
until this sudden check threw all their crews
out of employment. Strange to say, the very
next day the crisis came to an end. I am
afraid my readers will be shocked when I
tell them the extraordinary manner in which
this was brought to pass; nevertheless the
truth must be told, but I cannot justify the
course pursued. A butcher on board an Indiaman, much addicted to drinking, had committed
suicide just at this time. As no way out of
the trade dilemma presented itself, the following expedient was hit upon by the Europeans.
The dead body of the butcher was sent to the
Celestials, with a message to the effect that
he was so overcome with grief at having
caused the Chinaman's death, and so unable
to forgive himself, that he had put an end to
his life. The mandarins being perfectly satisfied with this explanation, trade was resumed
as usual.

CHAPTER XIII.

RETURN now to tell what was taking place on my own ship. Very soon all the spare cabins were taken up by merchants, chiefly Americans, who, feeling safer afloat than ashore, carried on their business correspondence there for over two years, whilst awaiting a settlement between the. Chinese government and the different nationalities. This freedom from the toil of a sea-going ship brought me in daily contact with a variety of characters. Amongst them was a Mr. Stanhope, with his friend Captain Hart, an adventurer whose exploits would fill a volume! He commanded a sloop, a one-masted cutter, about sixty tons, called the *Lampton*—a yacht formerly belonging to the Earl of Durham. He was cruising about the Navigator or Samoa Islands, the Fiji, the New Hebrides, etc., chiefly in quest of pearls, shells, bêche-le-mer, trepang and birds' nests for the China market.

The whole of the Sandwich group of islands has been formed by volcanic eruptions—by far the largest and most extensive in the world. Miss Isabella Bird gives an account of her visit to a vast open crater where the flames of fire were ascending to the height of from four hundred to six hundred feet, and continuously sending out lava which flowed to a distance of forty miles into the sea. It may be added that this lady ascended to a height of ten thousand feet. She found that water boiled on the summit at a temperature of 193° F., but tea could not be made, and it took twelve hours to boil a piece of pork. The climate on this group is said to be the finest in the world. One terrible malady, however, affects the inhabitants of all the islands alike—the leprosy—for which no remedy has ever been found. The persons suffering with it are kept separate at Molokai, where the number of lepers is said to be never less than seven hundred.

Now to return to Captain Hart. A strange adventure occurred while anchoring off one of these islands, which at that time was not marked in any chart or map. One night a canoe came alongside of the *Lampton*, its sole occupant being a white man, who related to the captain the following sad story. He had belonged to a ship which was trading in those parts for sperm oil, when she was unfortunately wrecked on the shore of that island. The natives, seeing their distress, decoyed the crew on shore, and foully murdered them all except himself, whom they spared on condition that he would become their Chief. When the captain heard of this treacherous conduct, he vowed vengeance, and landing next morning with some of his men, he shot every man on the island, leaving only the women and children alive. Mr. Adams, the survivor just alluded to, was a fine handsome man, with whom I became so well acquainted in after years that I entrusted him with the command of one of my ships. He communicated to me the details of his marvellous preservation, which fully confirmed the account I had heard in Hong Kong from Captain Hart. The lady who afterwards became his wife was personally known to me. They had become engaged before he left England, and the tidings of the wreck of his vessel, with the loss of all on board, plunged her into the deepest grief. On his return home two years later, he found her attired in the habiliments of mourning, which, however, were quickly exchanged for the ornaments of a bride! Verily truth is stranger than fiction! He was tattooed all over his neck and chest, being compelled to submit to this ungraceful decoration in order ;to save his life, the savages in this manner making him one of themselves; but he resolutely refused to allow his face and hands to be tattooed. Strange as this story is, I can vouch for the truth of it.

While anchored at Hong Kong, I had a Chinese cook, steward, and excellent servants on board, recommended by the resident Euro-peans who had left Canton and Macao for the former port. One of these latter pre-sented me with a beautiful China dinner service. We always kept a good table; our visitors were most abstemious as regards wine and spirits, paying me well for their quarters.

As the Chinese were continually threatening to exterminate or drive away the foreigners, a war ship, the *Hyacinth*, Captain Smith, was sent out from England to protect the fleet lying at Hong Kong. Whilst matters between us were still awaiting a settlement, I remember on one occasion that several war junks came from the Yellow Sea to engage the *Hyacinth*. This was only a ten-gun vessel, but she was

more than a match for all the naval force
the enemy could muster; indeed, the disparity
was perfectly ridiculous. Three war junks,
mostly composed of bamboo, having mats for
sails, with a few cannonade guns on board
each fixed in the vessel sides, and thus rendered
partially useless, represented the Chinese fleet;
added to which they were so crowded with
men that they trod one upon another, and
whether they were soldiers or sailors it was
impossible to distinguish. These junks were
set in a line of defence, upon which the
Hyacinth got under weigh, and commenced
the attack by firing two shots over their heads!
Immediately on perceiving that a well-directed
broadside from the *Hyacinth* would send them to
the bottom, the crews, one and all, skedaddled,
jumping into the water and escaping to the
shore. The English were too magnanimous
to pursue them, deeming it both merciless
and cowardly to fight with so feeble a foe.
The *Hyacinth* returned to her anchorage and
the war junks to Pekin, the latter reporting
that the barbarians ran away, and that they
were the victors!

The result of this encounter inspired us
with such confidence that we no longer
dreaded an attack. Although not in China

I

when Canton was bombarded, I have been informed that a small squadron of gun-boats opened fire on the city, which would very quickly have been in a blaze had not the terrified inhabitants hoisted a flag of truce and inquired on what terms peace could be purchased. The payment of three million dollars was the condition we offered. To this demand they readily acceded, and—will it be credited?—within two days this enormous sum was raised, and a treaty of peace signed, thus making short work of the strife. The prompt adoption of strong measures often prevents much slaughter, either in the case of Celestials or other peoples, since the display of superior power has the salutary effect of changing lions into lambs.

An understanding having been arrived at between our own Government and the Chinese, things became more settled, and we soon obtained a cargo. After the *Heroine* was loaded, it was my difficult task to engage officers and a miscellaneous crew for the voyage to London. I had commanded this ship to the satisfaction of the owner, who was on board the whole time we were lying at Hong Kong. He and I were on the best of terms, and I recollect his observing that

my whole heart and soul were in the work
of preparation to return home to England.
There was no Lloyd's agent to survey the
vessel; this duty, therefore, devolved upon two
ships' captains, who knew no more about the
hull of a ship than I did.   I was fully aware
that the *Heroine* had been laid up five years
altogether in India and China; no one knew
her age, and sometimes I had my suspicions
about the soundness of her timbers.   To add
to our difficulty, there were no dry docks here
for examining the state of boats and treenails,
but a coating of paint soon covered up all
defects.

The monsoon was not favourable for the
China Sea passage, we therefore came through
the Straits of Barselene into the Mindora
Sea, and thence into the South Pacific through
the Celebes Sea, Zuloo Sea, the Straits of
Salayer, and Macassar, a Dutch settlement
near Celebes.

We experienced calms, light winds, and a
long passage, obliging us to put into a port
on New Guinea for water, wood, and provisions.   Here we found plenty of sago, turtles
in abundance, the bird of paradise, and
pigeons four times the size of ours.   We were
anchored on the Equinoctial line, and at the

very time of the sun's passing the Equator, consequently there was no shadow at noon-day. The mop-headed Papuas were cannibals at that time, though they were friendly to us and especially towards the Malay sailors on board. I am happy to say that missionaries have since visited this place with the Gospel, and many of the Papuas now sing praises to the God of salvation. The harbour was very safe, the surroundings magnificent, and nothing vile but man. Indeed, the scenery here is far beyond my power of description. The natives call the place Waygion, and the bay, which is from three to four miles in circumference, is in the form of a horse-shoe, with a white sandy beach, and a river of fresh water running round it. The centre of the bay is studded with numerous small islets; these are decked with the brightest foliage down to the very edge of the sea, presenting the appearance of beautiful bouquets in the water. The neighbouring hills and forests are grand in the extreme, and I can unhesitatingly assert that this spot is the fairest I have ever looked upon.

It was in this bay that the French vessels anchored when in search of La Perouse, the French navigator, who, in 1785, was appointed to command a small squadron fitted out for a voyage of discovery round the world. His ships were never seen after leaving Botany Bay, January, 1788, and he and his men, no doubt, perished.

With the exception of firewood and water, our stores, such as beef, pork, and biscuits, for the remaining voyage, were exhausted; we therefore put into Batavia for supplies. Here the owner left the ship, to the great satisfaction of all on board. A very short time sufficed to take in what was required, and we proceeded through the Straits of Sunda, which separate Sumatra from Java, homeward bound.

CHAPTER XIV.

WE rounded the Cape of Good Hope in fine weather, and at length arrived at St. Helena for water, our stock being reduced to the last cask. On stepping into the boat to go off to Jamestown, the only landing place in the island, I perceived that one of the treenails in the top sides was rotten. This confirmed my former suspicion that the ship might prove very defective in meeting the storms of the North Atlantic Ocean. Having little opinion of their judgment, I did not consult with the officers, but after carefully weighing the matter over, I resolved to have the ship surveyed and repaired before proceeding further. This detained us some time, after which, feeling better satisfied, we again set sail. The ship was tight, and made little or no water until we arrived in, what is called by sailors, the " roaring forties "—that is, the latitude of 40° North. Here we were overtaken by a very heavy gale, or rather cyclone, which lasted three days. The ship laboured very much in the heavy seas which struck her continually. At last, and in the night, during an eclipse of the moon, a mountainous wave towering over all the rest, struck her, and although she rose up again above all, it must have loosened or separated the top sides from the bends. This is a weak part in old ships, being between light and loaded water-marks. Under the impression that she was likely to go down, the mizzen mast was cut away with all the gear, spars and rigging attached to it. The ship put before the wind, and very fortunately the storm abated considerably. After a careful examination, it was deemed necessary to throw a great part of the cargo overboard, and save our lives by running before the wind for some safe port. We had a long distance to go, but the weather was very fine and favoured us until we came near to the land, when another severe storm overtook the *Heroine* in her disabled state and with a worn-out crew. I was intending to run into Gibraltar Bay, but not having been able to take any observation to correct our reckoning, we found the ship had been carried by an undercurrent towards the African side of the Straits. It was night, but I could see the sea breaking heavily on Cape Spartel; by and bye,

some one forward called out "breakers ahead!"
I ordered the helm to be put hard to star-
board; but whether the helmsman mistook the
order, or put the helm the wrong way, I cannot
say. It is more probable that, being partly
dismasted, the ship did not answer the helm,
and so struck on a sandbank. The gale
increased, and heavy seas soon dashed her to
pieces amidships, leaving the poop deck and
forecastle entire for the rest of the night. Five
of the Europeans, with myself and the chief
officer, Mr. McDougall, assembled on the poop-
deck, and held a prayer meeting in the midst of
the raging wind and furious waves, expecting
every moment to be dashed overboard. We
were not afraid to meet death, feeling sure that
as repentant sinners we should find acceptance
with God through our Lord Jesus Christ. I
afterwards lost sight of my companions in the
darkness of the night; they were all sober men,
and I had full confidence in their readiness to
render the best help they could. All night long
I could hear the Asiatics in prayer; their suffer-
ings must have been intense, on account of
their less robust physique. In the morning,
when daylight broke, many, alas! had disappeared. After watching a slant between the
billows, I went forward and sat down in the

PRAYER IN THE STORM.

fore chains, clinging to the rigging. Towards mid-day, the storm abated somewhat, when I ordered all to try to save themselves, entreating them not to trust to their swimming powers, but to pieces of the broken wreck which would support them through the surf; and I observed that all who heeded this caution arrived safely on shore. Towards evening the sea was a little smoother; I was the last man to leave the ship, which I did with a passenger, a young man who had been valet to Lord John Churchill, captain of H.M.S. *Druid*. We both stripped, and launching one of the deck planks, jumped into the sea on the lee side. A strong current was running past the wreck, the first sea that struck the plank carrying off the young man, who went down out of sight, leaving me alone to struggle with the waves. I picked up a sinking man who was clinging to a small broken piece of the wreck, and we both reached the shore in safety; but I was so exhausted that I fell down in attempting to walk, and was carried up into a tent; the first mate and the Europeans rejoicing to give me a greeting. It was two or three days before I fairly recovered this shock. The Consul-General, Mr. Drummond Hay, hearing of the wreck, came with provisions and help, bringing also a tent for

us to sleep in.   This is called the coast
of Barbary, and certainly "the Barbarians
showed us no little kindness, for they kindled a
fire and received us" with great hospitality.

I cannot conscientiously charge myself with
any want of seamanship as being the cause
of this terrible catastrophe.   In justice to myself,
I must say I believe the cause can be stated in
one sentence—the *Heroine* was a rotten ship, not
seaworthy; had she been otherwise, sound in
her timbers, and well fastened together with new
treenails, I should have delivered the cargo and
men all safe in London.   I have commanded
ships successfully for fifteen years; the sad story
just narrated records the only mishap I have
met with of any great consequence during the
whole of my sea-going experiences.

In leaving this painful episode, I beg the
reader to remember that I had twice saved the
ship, once in the Straits of Malacca, when she
was ashore, and the other time on the Hen and
Chickens bank, as she was running into a bay
with the palm trees nearly under her forefoot.

When Sunday came, the Consul-General conducted divine service under a tent.   I cannot
recollect a single person who was present, my
mind being so absorbed in the solemn service.
Not one opportunity of attending public worship

had been afforded me during the many years spent in India and China. Like a thirsty soul at the Fountain of Living Water, I drank in every word, unconscious of all around. The conviction that I was a vile and guilty sinner had never been forced upon my mind as it was then. There and then I determined to give up all my worldly companions, and thought to go "mourning all my days," but the "spirit of heaviness" was suddenly exchanged for "the garment of praise" (Isaiah lxi., 3). It was during the reading of the one hundredth Psalm—

"O be joyful in the Lord all ye lands ;
  Serve the Lord with gladness,
  And come before His presence with a song"—

that the Spirit of God brought me the message of salvation through faith in Christ Jesus, causing my soul to rejoice in God my Saviour. Life and light now entered my soul, dispelling all its doubts and fears. I was no longer a stranger to repentance and a godly sorrow for sin, and truly did I thank God for sending His Son to save sinners. This was the beginning of a new life, and never since that moment have I been oppressed with gloomy doubts or mournful frames. "Rejoice evermore," and "Pray without ceasing," are blessed injunctions, and should be counted as privileges by the soul whose "life is hid with Christ in God," and who is "kept by the power of God through faith unto salvation." I have no doubt that many men leave the hallowed influences of a happy home with the best intentions. All too quickly they meet with evil companions, who not only mock at religion, and break the Sabbath, but tempt them to do likewise ; thus the "good seed " sown early in the home is choked by "the lusts of other things entering in," and becomes unfruitful.

But "the pleasures of sin" are only "for a season "; soon comes the bitterness, the shame, and the sorrow, but the heart gets hardened, and the Lord has often to deal with the wanderer "by terrible things in righteousness." But He wounds only to heal, He smites to the ground only to raise up again whenever the wounded and bruised soul looks to Him in simple faith for pardon and salvation through our Lord Jesus Christ.

And here let me pause for a moment to speak of God's wonderful love, first in giving His only begotten Son "that whosoever believeth in Him should not perish, but have everlasting life," and then in His patiently waiting for and following after the wandering sheep. Oh! my reader, if you have not already sought His grace, lose no time "lest ye perish by the way." The best the world can give will never satisfy an immortal soul. I tried the broken cisterns, but they failed; now for many years I have tried Christ, and I can testify He " never faileth."

But to return to my narrative. My duty now was to save all the property connected with the wreck of the ship and cargo, and I had to look after a mixed gang of Jews, Christians, and Mahometans, in my efforts to rescue what I could from the devouring sea; and who can wonder when I say that the sight of a wrecked ship was continually before me for many a day?

From this scene I was removed to Tangiers in a small caravanserai or escort of mules and camels, and dwelt in the house of the Consul-General, Mrs. Drummond Hay showing me the greatest sympathy and kindness. During the three weeks I remained with them, I much enjoyed the family worship which we had night and morning, and believe it helped me forward in the spiritual life; God, by His grace, having preserved and kept me until now.

Lloyd's agent at Gibraltar sent a small vessel to take the tea saved from the wreck; this plan, however, proved a failure, as the

Governor, on hearing of it, issued an order forbidding any dealer to purchase or offer for sale damaged goods. When Mr. Drummond Hay was satisfied that everything had been done both properly and justly, he allowed me to proceed to Gibraltar, where I arrived after crossing the Straits in a leech boat. My first visit was to a tailor, from whom I ordered a suit of decent apparel, having since the wreck worn a suit belonging to the Consul, which gave me the appearance of a military man rather than a seaman. The agent for Lloyd's, Mr. Longlands Cowell, was a notary public, and I had to make before him a statement from memory of all the events of the voyage from Hong Kong to the time of the loss of the ship. The chief officer, with the petty officers, on their arrival in London were also called upon to make a similar statement before a notary public, and I heard that both narratives were in complete agreement with each other. It was necessary for these depositions to be taken before the owners could claim the insurances on ship and freight. There was at that time a barbarous provision existing in the Maritime Law of England, by which, in case of shipwreck, sailors were entitled to their wages up to the time of the disaster only, and precluded from claiming any afterwards. This was the rule—freight is the mother of wages—the safe arrival of the ship is the mother of freight,—so that poor Jack was often robbed of part of his earnings. I rejoice to say this custom was soon after abolished.

In my own case, after the owners of the *Heroine* had received payment in full of all their claims they snapped their fingers at mine, knowing that my documents and agreements were all lost, but this meanness and roguery was quite customary with that firm. After long and fruitless efforts to bring these tricky shipowners to a fair settlement, I relinquished the attempt in despair.

K

CHAPTER XIV.

AFTER an absence of ten years I thought it was time to go home and see my father, who lived in the West Riding of Yorkshire, near Doncaster. He was then in his eightieth year, having practised as a solicitor nearly sixty years! I related to him the history of my travels, showing that, from a financial point of view, I was no better off than when I left home, though I had gained invaluable experience. I had lost all my savings, but I had never lost that which I valued far more —my character and reputation. To his question as to what I was going to do in the future, I replied that I came home to see him, which was my duty, and to "raise the wind" in order to enable me to carry out a scheme which I had long cherished. This scheme he fully approved of when fairly laid before him. I had the reversionary interest on a legacy left me by an uncle, who had celebrated his golden wedding, and I found plenty of friends willing to advance what money I required. I gave strong and un- answerable reasons in favour of my new enterprise, which was to purchase part of a ship and take the command myself. My plea was this, I had worked many years for the benefit of others, and thought now the time was come when I might, with advantage, consider my own interest, instead of sailing in ships owned by other men, who realized all the profits of the voyages. My native air, combined with the renewal of early friend- ships and associations, and aided by my invariably temperate habits, soon restored me from the effects of the shock I had ex- perienced.

Very soon all that I wanted in the way of money was forthcoming, and even much more if I had needed it; being thus well supplied I was ready to start. A kindly feeling was the result of this renewal of old friendships, and once more I left home for London, accompanied by hearty congratulations, and indulging many bright anticipations for the time to come. Again I found myself in that great vortex of human life—the vast metropolis —where, fortunately, I was now not unknown.

With the experience of over ten years, I patiently waited—not for something to turn up, as formerly, but now upon the Lord, for "The Lord reigneth" was sufficient for me. Should not this truth be our confidence in every emergency?

I called on several shipowners, whom I knew to be most respectable men, stating my circumstances and proposal. They all expressed themselves as favourable to my undertaking, but informed me there was no employment in any trade for ships, commercial enterprise being very dull, and consequently the vessels were laid up, waiting a turn in the tide of events. I deposited my money, at call, in the London Joint Stock Bank, and shortly afterwards was offered the command of an emigrant ship, bound to Prince Edward Island in the Gulf of St. Lawrence. No partnership presented itself, and rather than be idle I accepted this offer. A considerable time was spent in the outfit, but at length we sailed from the London Docks. Although it was very late in the year for such a voyage with emigrants, I raised no objection, being pretty well acquainted with the North Atlantic, and also with the Gulf of St. Lawrence in the winter season. Before sailing, I had made up my mind, should the weather on the American side prove inauspicious, to land the passengers at Halifax, Nova Scotia, but I kept my own counsel. We had a very fine run across, indeed. Meeting with a homeward bound ship in a distressed state, I supplied her with stores, and ultimately we arrived on the Grand Bank of Newfoundland, when the winter season .set in with unusual rigour. We beat about day after day with gales alternating from north - west to south - west, until our masts, rigging and sails, were all more or less damaged; the ship's hull, however, was still staunch and strong. The passengers, especially the poor women and children, suffered extremely. At last I called the officers to-gether for consultation, and it was deemed expedient to bear up and run back for a port in the United Kingdom. When we had put the ship's stern to the gale, the passen-gers began to leap for joy, well knowing the difference between meeting the storm in the teeth, and running before the wind. In about twelve days we sighted the Fastnet Rock, off Cape Clear, on the south coast of Ireland, next day coming to an anchor in the Cove of Cork, now called Queenstown.

We had been out at sea fifty-seven days

. without once seeing land. It was Christmas Eve, and I went on shore and remained there all the next day. Several ships were lying in the port which had been obliged to do as we had done, the Cunard liners alone having been able to make their passage to New York, which was a little fur-ther south than our destination. The passengers were all in good health I am glad to say.

I must here relate what I saw on passing through a vigia, or shoal, in the midst of the ocean, as we were making for Cork. It was blowing furiously, the sea being contrary to the wind, causing the waves to leap up in wild agitation, sparkling with phosphoric light not unlike a gigantic caldron of boiling liquid fire. I knew we were all safe, the chart marking this spot as a very small one indeed. I mounted the rigging and looked all around. The brightness of the sea seemed to illumine the atmosphere as far as the eye could reach ; but it only lasted half-an-hour, after which we came into smoother water.

To resume my story. On arriving at Cork, the agent of the ship, with whom I resided for a day or two, came on board with Lloyd's agent, and a survey was held. The jury masts were condemned, much of the bulwarks found damaged, and stanchions stove in by the force

RUNNING BEFORE THE WIND.

of the sea, but the hull was sound and did not require to be docked. I had to make a protest before a notary, who copied from the log-book all the casualities entered there, which I had carefully noted on account of the insurance. Then followed the old story, familiar to most captains—one by one all the sailors left the ship. However, the carpenters and riggers set to work, and soon we were all prepared for sea again; but it was decided that the emigrants should remain on board until April, when the ice in the St. Lawrence would be broken up. One of the passengers acted as steward. I spent most of the time either at an hotel—the "Navy Arms "—or with friends, only taking luncheon on board, and thoroughly enjoying this break, which was a real rest to me.

Just as we were on the point of sailing, the ship was seized for debt by the mortgagee, and ordered back again to London, emigrants and all. I was asked to take the command again, although I had left the ship, and was living at the hotel. The agent was unable to meet with another commander to take charge of the vessel, engage a new crew, and return to the London Docks, which we had left the previous November; so I consented to do so, stipulating payment before sailing.

In one week the voyage was accomplished, and then the mortgagee put his own ship-keeper on board. The emigrants applied to the Lord Mayor, Alderman Humphreys. I was summoned to show cause why I had not fulfilled my agreement, made before sailing, to land the passengers at Prince Edward Island. I attended at the Mansion House, where most of the emigrants were assembled. His lordship in opening the case, reminded me that I had incurred a penalty of one thousand pounds for not landing the emigrants at the port in America, for which the ship had cleared out at the Custom House in London. My reply was, "My lord, I am quite aware of it, and am ready to carry out my part whenever the Company is prepared to find a ship for the purpose." The emigrants said they did not wish to press their charge against the captain, who had always treated them with much kindness and consideration. Then the bubble burst—one of the emigrants remarking that the company, who had promised them grants of land, had not so much as would bury them if they had arrived there. I discovered afterwards that the whole scheme was hatched in White Cross Street Prison by designing men of no character, who had got

the names of well-known and highly respectable
men on a flaming prospectus, and launched it
before the needy ones, who were willing to
emigrate under favourable auspices.

A long article appeared next day in the
Morning Chronicle, complimentary to myself,
as showing a laudable disposition not to
conceal any facts touching the misadventure.
A cheque for fifty pounds was sent anony-
mously for the benefit of those who had been
so shamefully deceived, and an offer of assistance to any who wished still to emigrate, which
offer not one would accept, the Atlantic waves
proving a sufficient barrier to keep them on
this side of the ocean. How these schemers
had contrived to keep up the delusion so
long was always a great puzzle to me, and
when their fraudulent dealings were exposed
to the public, I could not but congratulate
myself that I had not been one of their dupes.

Amid the varied circumstances of our chequered
life let us trace God's faithfulness in smoothing
our path, and learn to trust Him in the future.

The deadlock in the shipping continued some
time longer, but I comforted myself, remembering the Persian proverb, " Everything comes
to the man who knows how to wait." As it
was my intention to purchase a ship, or part

of one, it was necessary to keep on the look-out; and having consulted a friend, a retired shipbuilder, who was well known to be a good judge of all kinds of craft, he recommended a vessel which he knew to be faithfully built and a good carrier, advising me on no account to be in a hurry, and adding that soon I should be able to get her at my own price.

Meanwhile, two gentlemen who had been shipowners sent for me, asking if I knew anything about guano. I replied in the affirmative, having seen ships discharging it in the London docks; it was said to be worth twenty shillings per cwt., and was then used only for horticultural purposes. One of them said he had seen his broker, who offered a charter to some port south of the Equator, with sealed orders to be opened on arrival there. He offered me the command of the vessel, *Frances Lawson*, which I accepted, thinking I could perceive a rift in the dark cloud so long hanging over the shipping interest.

This merchant came from Liverpool to London—a fact which raised my suspicion that there was something in the wind, though the secret was unknown, and I began to fit out the *Frances Lawson* for the projected passage to the Equator with sealed orders.

By this time I had completed the purchase of *La bonne mère*, a plantation-built ship of black birch and juniper wood, just what I desired, with the ownership and command. But I could not break an agreement, so I sailed in the former, a captain being appointed to the latter, who was directed to sail for the same parts as we were bound for. Before leaving, I called one day to purchase an Admiralty chart of a section of the coast of South Africa, which, though strictly belonging to the Admiralty, they do not refuse to sell to the captain of a merchant ship making an application. I found that others had been inquiring for the same charts, thus confirming my previous impression that there was some enterprise going forward in that part of the world.

Shakespeare says, "There is a tide in the affairs of men, which, taken at the flood, leads on to fortune." I began to think after my two late misadventures that the current of events was about to change in my favour, which ultimately proved to be the case. I once more set sail; full of hope, and impressed with the idea that should the undertaking prove successful, I might look forward to an early retirement. We got nicely down the Thames, and came to anchor in the Downs.

CHAPTER XV

EARLY the next morning, it being very bright, with a fair wind, we were proceeding down the English Channel, when a collision (one of the most stupid I ever knew) took place, at eight o'clock, in the following manner: the steersman on a brig called the *Halifax*, put his helm the wrong way, and dashed into my ship. I was below at the time, winding up the chronometer. The brig sheered off with very considerable damage. The *Frances Lawson* looked like a wreck; the quarter-boat was smashed, the steering apparatus carried away, mizzen gaff, main-top gallant-yard, taff-rail and quarter-piece stove in—exposing the timbers; but all the injury was, fortunately, above the water mark. On recovering from the fright, I saw the other ship's name, and bore up for the Downs. In a few moments I regained my self-possession, and giving the word, " Bear up again and run down the Channel," we all set to work with

a good will to repair the ship, and by eight
o'clock in the evening she was seaworthy.   In
this short interval we had made a new wheel,
scarped the broken spars, covered the taff-rail
in, and placed the jolly-boat in board, smashed
as it was.

A second misfortune followed close upon
this.   In crossing the Bay of Biscay, I was
aroused early one morning by these words,
" Please, sir, the bowsprit is in two halves."
This is one of the most serious accidents that
can happen to a ship at sea.   The weather
continuing fine, favoured our position, though
the carpenters and men seemed paralyzed.   I
thought we must shorten all sail on the foremast, and run for Bilboa.   Never before had
I experienced two such disasters—a collision,
and the loss of the principal spar in the ship,
which secures the mast and rigging.   Having
a long day before us, I directed the carpenters
to cut away a part of the " knight-heads,"
slip two broad planks on their edges inboard
and outboard, frap stout chains round the
fishes, binding all tightly together, drive in
some oak wedges, and set up the rigging and
bobstays.   All this was well accomplished before
nightfall, and though unsightly enough, it lasted
the whole voyage, and was stronger than the

original bowsprit. I am pleased to say that this casualty proved to be the last; and though I continued for five subsequent years to sail to different parts of the world, I met with no such mishaps again. On our return home the owner brought an action against the ship *Halifax*, and recovered eighty pounds damages.

The provisions supplied in the *Frances Lawson* were of very inferior quality. I remonstrated with the owner before we started, and used all my persuasive powers, remarking that not only would the men have to provide a cargo, which was unusual, but the mistaken economy might thwart the enterprise. He was, however, a pig-headed man, and refused to listen to my advice. I invariably stood out for the rights of poor Jack, being able to sympathize with him from having personally experienced his lot, indeed, a mutual understanding existed between us, and I was always on the best of terms with my crew. The salt beef was unfit for consumption, therefore I ordered it to be thrown overboard, and purchased the best I could meet with, paying double price.

On cur safe arrival at the Equator I opened the despatches in presence of both officers and found our conjectures, as to destination, were correct, Angra Pequina, at that time a *terra incognita*, being the port. A small sketch I had with me of the appearance of the land was most useful to us, and we anchored in a safe bay.

The discovery of guano on the south-west coast of Africa—a discovery inferior to none in this century, not excepting even that of gold in California and South Australia, has proved to be one of the greatest benefits to agriculture. There is an old Latin proverb, which says, " *Effadiuntur opes, irritamenta malorum.*" (Riches, the incentives to vice, are dug out of the earth.) But guano has proved an excellent incentive to the productiveness of the soil exhausted by constant cropping. Chemical analysis showed it to be worth ten pounds per ton, and the entire deposit five millions sterling. Guano has proved the source of wealth to this country to the amount of millions of money.

Now I must boast myself a little. I was at Angra Pequina in the first ship when there was only one other there besides mine, and I took the first cargo up the English Channel to Hull that was ever imported from Africa. On my second voyage, I found five hundred ships were loading on the coast. When I was half loaded *La bonne mère* came in, and,

L

knowing there was an abundant supply of the deposit at Ichaboe, I despatched the captain there. Both ships were soon fully loaded, and arrived safely in Hull.

The two cargoes were very readily disposed of, enabling myself and partner to purchase a new ship, which we named *Young England*. I could now call myself a shipowner, and I sailed again in command of the new vessel, while Captain Adams, before alluded to, went in *La bonne mère*, both of us bound for Ichaboe, and both returning home safe to Liverpool with full cargoes; the cargo of *Young England* being valued at five thousand pounds. Immediately I set sail again for the same object, exchanging the *Young England* for *La bonne mère*, but in the interval the islands had all been completely cleared. I imagine that one thousand ships had loaded there, carrying on an average five hundred tons each, so that half a million tons of the deposit must have been removed.

Having forseen what would happen when this El Dorado was exhausted, I had taken a supply of goods to barter with the Africans for a cargo of dye-woods, and other productions. After sailing the whole length of the south-west coast of Africa, from Ichaboe to the

"LA BONNE MERE" IN SEARCH OF AN "EL DORADO."

Cammeroons, in a fruitless search after nitrate of soda, visiting Port Alexander, Walweck Bay, Great Fish Bay, Hollam's Bird Island, Mercury Island, and other places, I finally opened trade with the natives in the river Gaboon.

While searching along the coast at Port Alexander, I found, six inches below the surface of the sand, a layer of some substance resembling nitrate of soda. It was as white as loaf sugar, melted in water, leaving little or no residuum, was without taste, and fire had no effect upon it. A sample brought home was pronounced to be " salt that had lost its savour."

Near the Equator the rains continue ten months in the year, during which season it is very unhealthy, the rainfall measuring fourteen feet per annum ; happily we were there the two months of fine weather.

Before proceeding to narrate my trading experiences in the Gaboon, let me mention an incident which occurred at this time. Whilst coasting along the sandy desert, we met with the Bosjesmans, two of whom remained in the ship for several days. A French vessel, then in the river, had a fine gorilla on board, and I had thus an opportunity of observing the apparent similarity between these degraded specimens of the human family and the gorilla. Both my officers and the super-cargo persistently affirmed the latter to be the better looking, and declared that we all sprang from the apes! While expatiating on the folly of such reasoning, I pointed out to them one of these men, and showed them he evidently had some idea of a Supreme Being—his body was mutilated, one eye had been put out, two joints of one of his fingers were cut off, and a front tooth knocked out, and concluded by adding that " Man is a cooking animal, a decorative animal, and above all, a worshipping animal." Upon this, the poor savage, perceiving he was the ·subject of our discussion, pointed his hand upwards towards the sky. This significant gesture proved I had the best of the argument, showing as it did, that he had mutilated his body for the sake of his soul.

Now to resume my story. The goods which I had to barter with were cotton piece goods, rumauls or handkerchiefs, hatchets, matchets, tobacco in leaf, beads, looking-glasses, all of the commonest description, but suitable for the trade in Central Africa. This was quite a new feature in my experience as commander of a merchant ship. I resolved, however, to make the best of it, having failed to find any

fresh nitrate beds. The first question the wily
natives put to me, was, "Have you ever been
in this trade before?" to which I replied
that I knew the African coast well, but had
never before anchored in that port. Some
time elapsed ere we came to an understanding,
as I found King Jackeromandy and his tribe
hostile; therefore, I removed to the river
Danger. Here, a man (who spoke good
English), calling himself Peter, son of King
George, came on board and warned me of the
hostile tribes. We soon entered into negocia-
tions with several kings or chiefs of villages,
King Quaqus, King Kella, King Jim, and others.
Some of those chiefs assumed a dignity be-
fitting their lofty titles, when paying a visit
with their trains of wives, and expected to be
received by a royal salute of cannonades or
small guns. I submitted to this custom, and
presented their Majesties, as they expected me
to do, with a "dash" or present, consisting
of samples of the articles I had for traffic.
I found in this trade of barter, I was to give
the goods before receiving their equivalent,
and they made several attempts to cheat, but
as I never retaliated, a good understanding
was soon established between us. One day
we missed several articles of value from the

vessel, so the next morning I caught the first three men I could lay hands on, and hand-cuffed them together. A great palaver ensued, and very soon the missing articles were restored. In matters of business there were some shrewd men amongst these natives, but after a few days experience I was a match for them all. The cleverest among them was King Richard, who had a withered hand, and a hump on his back; he always kept his fetish in his left hand, and to my enquiry why he did so, he replied, "No tiger, or lion, or gun, can injure me with this charm."

This conversation took place on shore where I seldom went; I had in my hand a double barrelled gun loaded, also some bullets in my pocket, and I said to King Richard: "You stand one hundred yards from me, and I will drill a hole through you." His answer was, "My fetish is not for white man's gun."

When he first came on board he brought a cocked hat and a naval uniform under his arm, apologizing for not wearing them on account of the great heat, his only covering being a loin garment. All the wives and daughters of the other kings appeared in the same costume.

I was most careful to keep my sailors

entirely separate from the traders, employing natives to bring the cargo on board, whilst I occupied my men in duties on the ship. We lived well, enjoying the poultry, young goats, plantain fritters, and occasionally cabbage from the tree of that name; the latter is the sweetest vegetable I ever tasted, something like kale, but with an almond flavour. The working hours were from ten to four, then I drove my visitors all ashore, and was glad to rest from this fatiguing employment of bartering. With them, time was no object, for they were ready to palaver half-a-day over every bargain, but I assured them my time was worth a guinea a minute, and I used all the dispatch I could. In about one month a full and complete cargo was obtained, when we returned to Liverpool without any casualty, or incident worth recording.

CHAPTER XVI.

ARRIVING at Liverpool, I found to my surprise that my partner was living *incognito*, having been speculating with a Liverpool man of no reputation—a dangerous and desperate adventurer, as I had always heard him to be. Between them, they purchased a large ship called the *Providence*, and urged me to join with them, which I persistently refused to do. I had made three successive voyages to Africa, and brought home three full cargoes in a little over eighteen months. The Liverpool merchants did their utmost to persuade me to remain in the African trade, as being the most profitable, but I refused every overture. One idea now took possession of my mind—how to free myself from this undesirable partnership. I was then suffering from overwork, as well as from the effects of the deleterious African climate on the last trip, so I sold my share in the *Young England*, and acting on medical advice, I retired to a farm-house in the country for nine months. My ship, *La bonne mère*, was on her voyage to the west coast of South America. As to the two speculators, I will make a short story of their career. Their ship, *Providence*, met with repeated accidents, one close upon another, which ultimately ruined them. It would take several pages to relate the tissue of misadventures unparalled in my experience which led to this. Yet after all the ship came home with bottomry and respondentia bonds, claimed by shipwrights for repairs done in Quebec. To make it clearer, the ship and cargo were pledged for repairs, giving the ship-wrights a claim on both until their bills were paid. The two speculators went through the Bankruptcy Court, assets nil. This unhappy termination of their enterprise only served to strengthen my resolve to avoid a partnership for the future, as I found it often meant nothing more than a staff for an imprudent or a dishonest man to lean upon ; and remembering, also, how nearly I had been drawn into this vortex, I felt thankful indeed for my present unfettered position.

Time, with ceaseless but inaudible flight, passed swiftly on, and once more I found myself in London, in 1847, the year of the

Irish famine. There was " corn in Egypt," how-ever. *La bonne mère* had arrived with a cargo of goods from the Chincha Islands, and again I took the command, though the ownership meanwhile had changed hands. While walking one day in Commercial Road, I met an old shipmate, with whom I had sailed round Cape Horn. He was just the individual I wanted, and was the only godly man I had sailed with in twenty years! Hè was at that time out of employment, so I engaged him at once as carpenter.

The freights were very go d in the corn trade, so chartering *La bonne mère*, or the *Bonnie Mary*, as the sailors used to call her, for Alexandria, we sailed immediately as there was no time to be lost, the high freight being a very tempting inducement. Sailing in the Mediterranean was like a pleasure trip to me; we made a quick passage out with favourable weather, and I took the ship into the harbour when we came to anchor. While sitting at breakfast that morning, I felt a peculiar vibration run through the vessel, and exclaimed, " We are aground!" I flew on deck to ascertain the cause, when a man who was coming from shore to us in a boat called out, " Did you feel the shock of an earthquake ? " Several houses were thrown down in the town, and at Cairo much mischief was done to buildings.

I may relate, *en passant*, that my butcher at Alexandria who supplied me with a fat sheep every other day, was called Mahomet. He told me his father piloted Nelson's fleet into Aboukir Bay before the battle of the Nile, and that the Admiral threatened him with the loss of his head if any of the ships touched the rock.

After finding the consignee we commenced loading, and in order to preserve every grain of the precious cargo from damage, I myself laid all the dunnage and matting, making also a wall amidship to prevent the grain from shifting during the voyage homewards. When we had completed loading and were ready for sea, I found myself in a dilemma from which nothing but tact, courage, and promptitude could extricate me. The ship had sprung a leak! How to proceed on the voyage was a problem difficult to solve. To discharge the cargo and repair would involve an immense loss. I heard one man say with an oath the *Bonnie Mary* would never reach London! but I turned on my heel and took no notice of his remark. It was, however, a warning to use every precaution possible, and not to underrate the risks of the position.

Having no opinion of my officers' judgment, I consulted in private with my old, staunch friend the carpenter, pointing out to him that I entertained no doubt about the soundness of the ship, and felt assured that when we got out into the Mediterranean she would take up, *i.e.*, her outside planks would swell and she would become tighter. To this he agreed, adding that if I felt disposed to risk it, he was quite willing to help. How to deal with the sailors was our next difficulty. I proposed giving them an advance of money and liberty to go on shore to make their purchases for the voyage, with this strict injunction, that every man was to be on board by six o'clock the next morning, adding that then I should set sail and go to sea. I made no allusion to the leaky state of the vessel.

All this was carried out successfully; on the following morning I called out, "Are you all on board? Where is the carpenter?" The answer came, "Below in the forepeak, stopping the leak." Not a word more was said; without a pilot we made sail and proceeded homewards, the weather being invitingly fine and favourable.

> " With the blue above, and the blue below,
>   We speeded on merrily."

The ship took up a little, but the leak was only partially stopped, it being a difficult matter to stop a leak from the inside. Still, in order to keep all dry, I had the pumps attended to carefully every four hours, day and night, all the way home.

We called at Cork for orders, and found our destination was Gloucester, where I delivered the cargo without a handful of damage. When paying the men their well-earned wages, I made a mistake, giving to one of them two five-pound notes instead of one, not having the usual clerk with me on this occasion. He returned and showed me his money, it was quite true. I mention this because it was the same man whom I had heard say with a dreadful oath in Alexandria that the ship would never reach London. I never allowed swearing on board, and do not remember hearing it except then.

On my return home I was asked by a friend, " Did you find your money in the sack's mouth ? " I answered, " No, I did not, but I made a sackful of money." All I wanted now was a fair field and no favour. The *Bonnie Mary* was sold, and I bought her in, laying her up for the winter in Gloucester docks.

In the spring of the following year, I made a voyage to St. John's, New Brunswick, and later on another to Quebec; both voyages were profitable I am thankful to say. After this I retired from going to sea, employing other captains to take charge of my vessels.

Thus from cabin-boy I rose to be captain, climbing slowly step by step up the ladder to independence. I became a member of Lloyd's, in the Royal Exchange, for the insurance of ships and merchandize, a member of the Royal Agricultural Society, a member of the Ac-climatization Society, shipowner, supercargo, and ship's husband.

I cannot conclude my story of twenty-five years of sea-faring life without again testifying to the faithfulness of Him whose preserving care I have so abundantly experienced. And now, with the sincere desire that my readers may derive both interest and profit from this narrative, I send it forth; praying also that they may taste for themselves the blessedness of those "who know the joyful sound" of "the Gospel of the grace of God."